LANCASHIRE COUNTY LIBRARY

PRINCE NADIR'S
SECRET HEIR

PRINCE NADIR'S SECRET HEIR

BY

MICHELLE CONDER

MILLS
BOON®

First published in Great Britain 2015
by Mills & Boon, an imprint of Harlequin (UK) Limited,
Large Print edition 2015
Eton House, 18-24 Paradise Road,
Richmond, Surrey, TW9 1SR

© 2015 Michelle Conder

ISBN: 978-0-263-25654-3

Printed and bound in Great Britain
by CPI Antony Rowe, Chippenham, Wiltshire

For Pam Austin, who planned the most wonderful holiday while I wrote this book. Meeting you on that train ride to Paris was one of life's little gifts.

And for Paul for always being there.

CHAPTER ONE

SOME DAYS STARTED out well and stayed that way. Others started out well and rapidly deteriorated.

This day, Nadir Zaman Al-Darkhan, Crown Prince of Bakaan, decided as he stared at a very large and very ugly statue squatting in the corner of his London office, was rapidly sliding towards the latter. 'What the hell is that?'

He glanced over his shoulder at his new PA, who blinked back at him like a newly hatched owl transfixed by a wicked wolf. She'd been recommended by his old PA, whose recently acquired husband had taken offence at the seventeen-hour work-days Nadir habitually kept, and he wasn't sure how she was going to work out.

In general people either treated him with deference or fear. According to his brother, it had something to do with the vibe he gave off. Apparently he emanated an aura of power and ruthless determination that didn't bode well for his personal relationships, which was why he didn't have many. Nadir had merely shrugged when Zach had delivered that piece of news. Personal relationships ranked well down below work, exercise, sex and sleep.

Not always, a sneaky voice whispered in his ear and he frowned as that voice conjured up an image of a woman he had once briefly dated over a year ago and had never seen since.

'I believe it's a golden stag, sir,' his PA all but stuttered, definitely falling into the fearful category.

Applying some of that ruthlessness his brother had mentioned, Nadir banished the image of the blonde dancer from his mind and turned back to the statue. He could see it was a stag and he only hoped it hadn't once been alive. 'I got that, Miss Fenton. What I should have said is—what the hell is it doing in my office?'

'It's a gift from the Sultan of Astiv.'

Ah, just what he needed—another gift from some world leader he didn't know, offering commiserations over the death of his father two weeks ago. He'd only been back in Europe a day since the funeral and he was, frankly, tired of the reminders which always brought up the fact that he felt nothing for the man who had sired him.

Annoyed, he strode across to his desk and sat down. His PA stopped in his doorway with her iPad clutched to her chest.

'Tell me, Miss Fenton. Should a person feel badly that their father has just passed away?'

His PA's eyes slowly widened as if he'd just raised a gun to her head. 'I couldn't quite say, sir.'

Meaning she didn't want to say. Which didn't surprise him. It wasn't as if he was known for seeking out the personal opinion of those who worked for him. Not on private matters anyway.

Still, he couldn't quite contain his frustration as his PA shuffled into his office and perched on the edge of an office chair. Between fear and awe he'd go with awe every time but his new PA looked as if she was waiting for him to attack her with a blunt instrument, which could have something to do with the whole host of unwanted emotions and memories his father's death had stirred up in him. He knew a shrink would tell him that was a good thing. As far as Nadir was concerned, long buried emotions and memories were long buried for a very good reason.

'What else have you got for me, Miss Fenton?'

She flashed him a relieved look that he had turned his mind to work. 'Miss Orla Kincaid left a message.'

Nadir already regretted calling up an old mistress to see if she was free for dinner. Earlier, when it had crossed his mind, he'd been bored by a group of business executives who couldn't give away a cold beer to a dying man in the desert let alone convince him to shell out millions to invest in a product they were trying to manufacture on the cheap. 'Let's have it.'

His PA shifted uncomfortably. 'She said—and I quote—"I'm only interested if he's going to take our relationship seriously this time"—unquote.'

Rolling his eyes, Nadir told her to strike that one. 'What else?'

'Your brother rang and wants you to call him ASAP.'

Maybe Zachim had received a giant stag as well. But more likely he wanted to know how Nadir was going with his plan to help haul their Arabic homeland into the twenty-first century. With a spaceship, Nadir thought wryly, or maybe a really big front-end loader. His father had ruled Bakaan with an iron fist and now that he was dead it was supposed to be Nadir's job to lead the country into the future. Something he had no intention of doing.

Years ago he had made a promise to his father that he would never return to rule Bakaan and Nadir always kept his promises. Fortunately, Zachim had been groomed in his stead and had agreed to take on the position as the next King of Bakaan. Poor bastard. 'Get him on the phone.'

'I have other messages,' she said, balancing her iPad with one hand.

'Email them to my palm pilot.'

Moments later his palm pilot beeped right after his landline. His new PA was efficient; he'd give her that at least.

'If you're going to hassle me over the business proposal to reinvent the Bakaani banking system I'd like to remind you that I do have an international business to run,' Nadir grouched good-naturedly. Despite the fact that they were only half-brothers, Zachim was the only person Nadir would call a true friend and they caught up whenever their work paths crossed.

'I wish it was only that.' His brother's tone was grim. 'You need to get back here right away.'

'Ten hours in that place was ten hours too long,' Nadir drawled. Before that he hadn't been back to Bakaan for twenty years and he'd be happy to make it another twenty. The memories his home-land conjured up in him were better left buried and it had been more of a battle to keep them at bay yesterday than he'd be willing to share with anyone. In fact the only way he'd succeeded was to call up images of that exotic dancer and he hadn't much liked thinking about her either. Es-pecially with the way things had ended between them. And here he was thinking about her again. He scrubbed a hand across his freshly shaven jaw.

'Yeah, well, you hotfooted it out of here before you heard the news,' his brother said.

Nadir lounged in his seat with a relaxed feline grace and propped his feet on his desk. 'What news?'

'Father named you the next in line to the throne. You're to be King and you better get your sorry arse back here quick smart. Some of the insur-gent mountain tribes are making moves to cause instability in the region and Bakaan needs a show of leadership.'

'Hold up.' Nadir's chair slammed forward as his feet dropped to the floor. 'Father named you the heir.'

'Verbally.' The frustration in Zach's voice was

clear. 'It seems that doesn't hold much sway with the council.'

'That's ridiculous.'

'That's what happens when you die of a heart attack without putting the paperwork in order.'

Nadir forced himself to relax and sucked in a deep breath. 'You know it makes sense that you become the next Sultan. Not only do you run the army but you've lived there most of your life.'

He heard his brother's weary sigh and hoped another lecture wasn't coming about how Nadir was the oldest and how it was his birthright. They'd discussed this ad nauseam for years but it was only yesterday that he'd realised Zach had always believed that he'd one day return to Bakaan and take over. 'I think you're making a mistake but you'll need to officially renounce your position to the council.'

'Fine. I'll send them an email.'

'In person.'

Nadir swore. 'That's ridiculous. This is the twenty-first century.'

'And, as you know, Bakaan is labouring somewhere around the mid-nineteenth.'

Nadir ground his jaw and picked up the stress ball on his desk, tossing it through the basketball hoop set up beside the Matisse on his wall. His father might not have planned to die when he had but he would have known the succession protocol. Was this his way of trying to control him from the grave? If it was, it wouldn't work. Once, when Nadir was a child, they might have had a close relationship but that had ended when Nadir realised how manipulative and self-centred his father was. 'Set it up for tomorrow.'

'Will do.'

He rang off and stared into space. That was what you got for not tying up loose ends at the right time. Twenty years ago he'd left Bakaan after his father had refused to give his mother and twin sister a state funeral after a fatal car accident. They had shamed him, his father had said, when they had tried to flee the country to start a new life. It didn't matter to his father that they had not lived as man and wife for years or that his mother and sister were desperately unhappy with their exiled life in Bakaan. It only mattered that they continued to live where his father had placed them. When Nadir had stood up for their honour his father had basically said it was either his way or the highway.

So Nadir had chosen the highway and his father

had disowned him. It was one of his old man's specialities—turning his back on anyone who displeased him—and Nadir had said *sayonara* and left to make his own way in the world. And it had been a relief because it helped him forget the role he'd inadvertently played in his mother and sister's deaths. It was also the last time he'd let his father manipulate him. Nadir had no doubt that not changing his will to reflect Zachim as the next leader had been a deliberate move on his father's part. But he wouldn't win.

Memories surged and Nadir cursed and rocked to his feet. He stared out of the window as a stream of sunlight broke through the clouds, casting a golden hue on the Houses of Parliament. The colour reminded him of Imogen Reid's long silky hair and his mood headed further south as he thought of her once more. She was another loose end he had yet to tie up, but at least with that one he had tried.

Frustrated with the way the day was turning out, Nadir thumbed through the messages his PA had sent to his palm pilot, his eyes snagging on one from his head of security.

A sixth sense—or more a *sick* sense—told him

his day was not about to take an upward swing just yet.

'Bjorn.'

'Boss-man.' His head of security spoke in a soft Bostonian drawl. 'You know that woman you asked me to track down fourteen months ago?'

Damn, he'd been right and every muscle in his body tensed. 'Yes.'

'I'm pretty sure we found her. I've just sent through an image to your handheld for you to check.'

Gut churning, Nadir pulled the phone from his ear and watched as the face of the beautiful Australian dancer who had haunted his thoughts for fourteen long months materialised on the screen. Fifteen months ago he'd met her at the Moulin Rouge after he and Zach had found themselves in Paris at the same time.

His brother had claimed he could do with seeing something pretty so they'd headed to the famous dance hall as a lark. Nadir had taken one look at the statuesque dancer with hair the colour of wheat and eyes the colour of a freshly mown lawn on a summer day and four hours later he'd had her up against the wall in his Parisian apartment with her incredible legs tightly wrapped around his lean hips. Then he'd had her on his dining room table, under his shower, and eventually in his bed. Their affair had been as hot as the Bakaani sun in August. Passionate. Intense. *All-consuming.*

He'd never felt such a strong pull to a woman before and even though his brain had warned him to back away he'd still made four consecutive unscheduled weekend trips to Paris just to be with her. Right then he should have known that she was trouble. That their affair was unlikely to end well. Little had he known it would end with him finding out she was pregnant and her claiming the child was his. Little did he know that she would then disappear before he'd have a chance to do anything about it.

Likely she'd disappeared because she *hadn't* been carrying his baby at all but still, the thought that he had fathered a child somewhere out in the world and didn't know about it ate away at him. A flush of heat stole over him. He didn't know what her game had been back then but there was no question that she had played him. He just wanted to know how much—and why. 'That's her. Where is she?' he bit out harshly.

'Turns out she's in London. Been here the whole time.'

'Any sign of a child?'

'None. Should I ask? I'm sitting inside the café she works at now.'

'No.' A welcome shot of rage pumped through Nadir's bloodstream, priming his muscles. It looked as if today was the day he was being given a chance to rid himself of all the irritating issues in his life and now that he thought about it that could only be a positive thing. A faint smile twisted his lips. 'That pleasure will be mine. Text me your location.'

'That guy looking at you is giving me the creeps.'

Tired from lack of sleep due to her teething five-month-old daughter, Imogen stifled a yawn and didn't bother turning towards the back of the room even though she knew who Jenny was referring to. He was giving her the creeps as well and not just because of his hard looks. She recognised him from somewhere but couldn't think where.

She folded a paper napkin at her station at the bar and darted another quick glance outside the café window to see if her housemate Minh had turned up. Her shift had already ended but she'd stayed back to help tidy up until he arrived.

Jenny elbowed her. 'I think he wants to ask you out.'

'It's the blonde hair. He probably thinks I'm easy.' Fifteen months ago she'd had an equally imposing male think the same thing of her but he'd been wearing a three-thousand-dollar suit and had completely charmed her. He'd also been a billionaire playboy with the attention span of a single-celled amoeba. She wasn't so gullible when it came to men now. And, anyway, this guy looked as if he belonged to the secret service or something. Which only made her feel more uneasy. The little retro café where she waitressed didn't usually attract the kind of clientele who required personal security, and she knew that the playboy in the three-thousand-dollar suit used to have his own detail. Was that where she had seen this guy before? With Nadir? It seemed impossible but, before she could dart another quick glance his way, Jenny nudged her.

'No need to worry now. I think I spot your boyfriend outside.'

Heat shot through Imogen's face and her head came up as for a split second she thought Jenny was referring to the playboy she'd never be able to forget, no matter how much she tried.

When she caught sight of Minh waving to her through the café window a whoosh of air left her lungs in relief. Boy, but she was jittery all of a sudden.

'I've never seen him before,' Jenny continued. 'And he looks so gorgeous carrying your little girl in that sling.' She sighed. 'I wish I could meet a man who was a looker and also a caring dad.'

Heart still pumping, Imogen waved to her friend and infant daughter. She guessed Minh was a looker with his exotic Eurasian tanned features and he was certainly one of the nicest men she had ever met in her life but she'd never seen him as anything other than a friend. And not just because he was gay but because Prince Nadir Zaman Al-Darkhan had not only left her with a baby to take care of but he'd also left her with a phobia about falling in love.

Well, maybe not a phobia, exactly. More a deep resolve to never let a man take advantage of her again. Her own father had taken advantage of her mother's inherent goodness and it had devastated Imogen to watch her mother make excuse after excuse as to why her father hardly ever spent any time with them.

'Your father works so hard, baby girl—he just needs time to relax, that's all.'

Relaxing with another woman and eventually leaving his wife for her? Imogen would never let that happen to her. If she ever attempted another relationship in the future she'd do so with eyes wide open and it would be on her terms and her terms only. A picture of Nadir's handsome face materialised in her mind and she pushed it away.

'Unfortunately, he's not my boyfriend.' Or her baby's father.

She threw Jenny a smile and wished her a fab Friday night out on the town before heading towards the back of the bar to grab her handbag and head out to meet her makeshift family.

Minh had been a godsend in more ways than one this past year. When she'd discovered she was pregnant her roommate, Minh's sister, had told her that her big brother was heading to America for six months and was looking for someone to housesit. With the lease coming up on their flat in Paris anyway, it had seemed like an opportunity straight out of the heavens and she'd jumped at the opportunity to look after his swanky Knightsbridge pad. But then she probably would have gone to Siberia if it meant getting out of Paris at that time.

With no close family to fall back on in Australia, she'd anticipated having time in London to lie low and sort herself out before the baby arrived. Unfortunately she hadn't reckoned on being so sick she could barely move from Minh's sofa the whole time. When Minh had returned home he'd taken her under his wing and told her she could stay for as long as she needed. He'd even visited her in the hospital right after her precious daughter had come into the world, while no doubt her baby's father had been wining and dining some supermodel on a tropical island or some such.

Imogen grimaced. She'd known about Nadir's reputation as a handsome rebel bad boy from the start and as far as she was concerned you could add irresponsible bastard to that list of seedy qualities as well. And maybe add stupidity to her own because at the time she'd imagined she had fallen in love with him. *Fool.*

To say she owed Minh a lot was an understatement. She especially owed him a chance to have his boyfriend move in with him without her and Nadeena cramping their style and she gratefully accepted the tips the barman passed to her on her way out. In another week or two she should have enough to look for her own place but she knew Minh wouldn't push. He had a heart as big as a mountain.

'Hey, gorgeous,' he said, kissing her cheek. 'How was work?'

'Fine.' She grabbed her smiling daughter out of his arms and planted kisses all over her upturned face. Nadeena stared up at her with Nadir's striking blue-grey eyes and ebony lashes. His smooth olive complexion. 'What have you two been up to?'

'I took her to the park and the outdoor café. I hope she's not smelly,' Minh said as he untied the baby sling. 'It's like holding a hot brick against you in this weather. And they complain London summers are tepid.'

Imogen laughed. 'One twenty-eight-degree day and you English are ready to call it quits. The trouble is that you don't know how to handle the heat.'

Minh gave her a droll look. 'The trouble is we don't *want* to handle it.'

Grinning, Imogen took the sling and slid it over her shoulders and settled Nadeena against her, all her earlier feelings of unease completely gone. She linked her arm through Minh's. 'You know how much I appreciate your help, right? I mean I can't thank you enough for babysitting today. Yesterday.' She made a face. 'Last week.'

'She's a darling child and the dodgy film I'm editing is still in the can. Until they call me back I'm a free man.'

'Don't let David hear you say you're a free man,' she teased.

About to give her some spunky reply, Minh's jaw fell open and nearly hit the pavement. 'Hold that thought,' he breathed in a stage whisper. 'The archangel of heaven has just landed and he's wearing Armani and a terrific scowl.'

Laughing at the theatrics he picked up from working with film stars, Imogen turned and her jaw not only hit the pavement, it continued all the way to Australia.

The ruthless, heartless bastard who had left her pregnant and alone in Paris was heading towards her, his long, loose-limbed strides eating up the pavement and scattering startled pedestrians like a shark mowing down a school of tuna.

Imogen's arms instinctively came up to wrap around a sleepy Nadeena, her mind completely blank.

Nadir stopped directly in front of her. 'Hello, Imogen.' As tall as she was, she still had to tilt her head back to look into his eyes that were currently shielded by aviator sunglasses reflecting her own stunned expression back at her. 'Remember me?'

Imogen was in such a state of shock at seeing him after only just thinking about him so vividly all her addled brain could come up with was how impossibly good-looking he was in his black suit. How tousled his midnight hair looked—no doubt from where he had run his fingers through it a hundred times already. Her own immediately itched to do the same thing and she curled them into the soft fabric of Nadeena's sling, disconcerted by the immediate and compelling effect he still had on her.

'I…of course.'

She swallowed heavily as his eyes dropped to Nadeena. The glint from his sunglasses made him look like a steely-eyed predator eyeing succulent prey. 'You had the baby.'

Something in the way he said that in his deep, smooth baritone that defied geographical distinction made the hairs stand up on the back of Imogen's neck.

It was the underlying anger, she decided. Maybe

even fury. And for the life of her she couldn't imagine why he should be so upset. *He* had left *her* fourteen months ago so didn't that mean she had the jump on anger right now? Unfortunately all she could conjure up was paralysed shock.

Sensing her unease, Minh shifted defensively beside her and Imogen took a deep breath, rallying her scattered senses. 'Yes.' She cleared her throat.

'That's nice.' Nadir's smile was all even white teeth and completely lethal. Then he slowly drew off his sunglasses and his shockingly beautiful blue-grey eyes drilled into hers with all the warmth of a glacier. 'Who's the father?'

CHAPTER TWO

WHO'S THE FATHER?

Imogen stared at Nadir, slowly digesting his snarled words. She'd only heard him use that tone once before and it was on the phone to some poor sod in his home country and the shock of it kick-started her brain into a usable gear. Steadying her trembling knees, she forced a smile to her lips and thought that of course he would want to know about the baby. Why wouldn't he? It was his doctor, after all, who had confirmed her pregnancy that fateful night in his Paris apartment all those months ago.

God, if she'd only left work five minutes earlier or later this whole situation might have been avoided. She swallowed heavily and forced herself to meet his hard stare, his raised eyebrow that could make him look either wickedly seductive or incredibly foreboding. Today it was definitely foreboding, which didn't help to explain the electrodes of excitement pulsing through her body, making her both shivery and hot at the same time.

No, not *excitement*, she corrected; it was *adrenaline*. Her fight or flight system was on overload; her reaction could hardly be considered excitement after the way he had treated her. The reminder of that helped calm her down and she gave him a tight smile, a deep sense of self-preservation warning her not to answer his question just yet. 'It's a surprise to see you like this.'

'I'm sure it is, *habibi*. Now answer my question.'

Swallowing heavily, she raised her chin. He used to whisper that term of endearment to her when he was about to seduce her and God, she wished it wasn't such an effort to hold those erotic memories of their fleeting time together at bay but it was. 'Why do you ask?'

'Don't play games with me, Imogen. I'm not in the mood.'

A ripple of unease slid down her spine and Minh, obviously sensing Nadir's ire as much as she could, half stepped in front of her. 'Ease up there, chief. There's no need to be aggressive.'

Nadir slowly turned his razor-sharp gaze to Minh and, although Minh didn't flinch, Imogen did. Unfortunately Minh had no idea that the infamous rebel prince was Nadeena's father. Imogen hadn't told anyone.

'And you are?' Nadir's question came out as if he'd just asked Minh if he had any last requests.

'Imogen's friend.'

'I suggest you back off, *Imogen's friend*.' Nadir's lip curled into a sneer. 'This is not your business.' Then he turned the full force of his attention back to her and Imogen really wished that he hadn't. 'Well?'

How could he make one word sound so powerful?

'Sorry, but I don't like your attitude, chief.' Minh puffed out his chest and Imogen groaned. 'You need to dial it down a little.'

'It's okay, Minh.' She gave his arm a squeeze, only just realising that her arm was still linked with his. 'I know him.'

Nadir pinned her with a patronising look. 'That's putting it mildly, *habibi*.'

His meaning was clear and Imogen felt a flush rise up her neck.

'I don't like him,' Minh said softly.

Neither did she but she drew on all her training as a performer and gave him a smile worthy of an award. 'It's okay. Really. Why don't you head home? I can take care of this.'

'You're sure?' Minh looked dubious.

'She just said she was, didn't she?'

Imogen only just managed to prevent Minh from trying to stand up to Nadir again and patted a sleepy Nadeena, who had grown restless. 'Go. Really. We'll be fine.'

'Call me if you need me,' Minh ordered, reluctantly heading towards Green Park tube station.

As soon as he was out of sight she let out a relieved breath. One hardcore male was better than two, wasn't it?

Reluctantly turning back, she calmed her breathing and faced Nadir. 'What's this about, Nadir?'

'What do you think?'

She tried to pull off a nonchalant shrug but her movements felt stiff and disjointed. He'd walked away from her fourteen months ago so she had no idea. 'If I knew I wouldn't ask,' she countered, slightly annoyed herself now.

His silvery gaze transmitted how unimpressed he was with her response. 'How old is she?'

'How do you know she's a she?' Imogen hedged.

'I don't think it's customary to dress a boy in a pink sunhat.'

'Maybe I'm just bucking the trend.'

His hissed breath held a wealth of reaching-the-end-of-his-tether impatience. 'How. Old. Is. She?'

Completely unprepared for both his anger and his relentless questioning, Imogen was at a loss as to how to follow the advice of her inner voice that warned her to tread cautiously and found herself blurting out the truth. 'Five months.'

He rocked back on his heels, his hands going to his waist and pushing his jacket back to reveal his broad chest. 'Then our affair did result in a child.'

Their affair? Talk about clarifying how he had felt about her back then… 'I didn't say that,' she retorted forcefully.

The words came out rushed and his eyebrows shot up. 'Then you *were* sleeping with someone else while we were together.' His voice held the tenor of a wounded bull, which didn't impress her at all.

'Trust you to take that line of thinking,' she said scathingly, remembering how he had basically accused her of the same thing their last night together in Paris. 'And it's none of your business.'

'If she's not mine then whose is she?' His gaze once again narrowed in on Nadeena.

'Mine,' she countered evenly.

Nadir's lips turned up into a snarl. 'Do you really think you can fob me off with semantics?'

Imogen felt a dull pain tweak behind her right eyebrow. After the way he had treated the news of her pregnancy, she wanted to know his current motivation before blurting out any more home truths. 'Look, Nadir—'

He said something in Arabic, cutting her off, and stepped closer to her, his wide shoulders blocking out all the natural light behind him. Imogen felt the cool glass of the shop window at her back and briefly closed her eyes to try and steady her racing heartbeat, only to snap them open again when Nadir's voice sounded way too close to her ear. 'Dammit, you're not going to faint, are you?'

Faint? Faint? She stared up at him and then darted her eyes to the side. No, she wasn't going to faint. But she did want to run. Fast.

'Uh-uh.' As if reading her thoughts, Nadir shook his head. 'You're not going to run again, Imogen, my sweet.'

Again? What was he talking about—*again?*

'I have no idea what you're talking about but I really need to go. I'm working another shift tonight.'

His eyes narrowed. 'Just so we're clear, *habibi,*'

he grated silkily, 'I have not searched for you for the past fourteen months to be given the run-around now.'

Imogen immediately felt hot and cold and then hot again and, just like the first time she had laid eyes on him, all the oxygen went out of the air—something that had almost been disastrous at the time as she'd been in the middle of performing the can-can in front of a full house. She'd noticed Nadir watching her almost straight away. He'd been sitting at a small front table with his brother—she'd later found out—but she had only had eyes for Nadir. And he for her, right up until the moment he'd found out she was *enceinte*.

As if sensing her distress, Nadeena stirred and shifted against her chest and Imogen tried to calm her nerves, if for no other reason than to keep Nadeena asleep.

Her first priority was to keep her daughter safe. Secure.

Not that she expected Nadir to hurt her physically. No, what she feared was his power to hurt her emotionally, which was often much worse because most bruises healed while mental scars remained for ever. Imogen knew because she had spent many years trying, and failing, to win her

father's love and she wasn't about to condemn
Nadeena to the same fate.

A picture of the secret service type in the café
came to her on a rush just as she caught sight
of him standing a little way off to the side. Had
Nadir been looking for her all this time? It seemed
impossible.

Her troubled eyes flew to Nadir and her ripple of unease ratcheted up to dread. 'Fourteen
months? What are you talking about?'

Noting the deep groove between Imogen's beautiful green eyes, Nadir instantly regretted his emotionally ragged outburst. What he needed to be
right now was cool and controlled. Finding her
with a child strapped to her body challenged that
considerably. As did her evasive attitude, which
implied that she had something to hide.

'We will not discuss this any further on the
street,' he decided. Apart from the fact that Imogen looked uncomfortably hot, it was also far too
public a place for this type of discussion. 'Come.'

'No.'

Haughty as ever, Nadir noted as he turned back
to her. He'd been attracted to that regal aspect of

her nature when they'd met. Now the trait annoyed him. As did her wide-eyed ingénue look.

Back when he'd first noticed her she'd seemed different from the other women who had adorned his life from time to time. Less artificial. More sincere. More genuine. Hell, he could laugh at that now. Imogen Reid had turned out to be as genuine as a whore with a hundred euros in her hand.

He glanced at the baby sleeping in her arms. Everything inside him said that she was his child and he wondered how much longer Imogen would have waited before turning up 'ta-da' style on his doorstep and demanding maintenance payments worthy of a queen. Not that it mattered. *He* had found *her* and that definitely gave him the upper hand.

And it mattered even less that her complexion had leached of all colour. These past months of not knowing if she had given birth to the child she had claimed was his, if she was okay, if the baby was okay, hell, if either one of them was even *alive* had eaten away at him. When she'd sent him a text telling him she had 'taken care of everything' he'd assumed she'd terminated the pregnancy. He'd felt sick at the thought but then knowing he'd got her pregnant in the first place hadn't exactly made him feel like dancing around a room.

Fatherhood wasn't something he'd ever contemplated before. Now it seemed that the fates had other ideas and if this woman had kept his child from him…deliberately… Callously…

He glanced at her. He didn't think he could like a person less if he tried.

'Nadir, please, if I…' She moistened her lips with the tip of her tongue. 'If I tell you that you're the father can we just leave it at that? Can we just…can we just part as friends?'

Nadir reeled. Was she serious? Because she couldn't possibly expect him to walk away from her after basically admitting the child was his with little more than *Have a nice life*. In fact, if he discovered that this child really was his then he wouldn't be walking away at all.

He stared down at her and noticed she had the look of a frightened mouse that had just been caught in a very large inescapable trap.

Apt, he thought—*very apt*. From the minute he'd laid eyes on her, his first instinct had been primal. He'd wanted to wrap her up and keep her. He'd wanted to brand her as his own. Disconcertingly, that urge was just as strong as ever.

He tugged on the collar of his shirt. Somehow, in the time between meeting her and now, he had lost his equilibrium and he wanted it back. Not even the thought of having to renounce the throne tomorrow affected him as deeply. Or maybe it was the combination of the two. 'I don't think you could have ever called us *friends*, Imogen.' Bed partners. Lovers. Now those fitted. Friends, not so much.

She looked up at him as if he'd just kicked a puppy. 'Good to know,' she said flatly, her pony-tail swinging around her shoulders as she made to move past him. 'Frankly, I don't know why you're even here.'

It was supposed to be her parting shot but Nadir moved so that once again he was directly in front of her.

'Come now, *habibi*. I know you're smarter than that.'

'Look, Nadir, the stand-over tactics are very intimidating. Well done you. But you can't stop me from walking away.'

He blew out a frustrated breath. 'If you'd cooperate and tell me what I want to know I wouldn't need to use any *tactics*. Now, my car is waiting at the corner.' He arched his arm towards a low-slung black beast of a Mercedes. 'Shall we?'

'No,' she bit out, 'we shall not. Not until I understand what this is about.'

The line between her brows reappeared as she stared at him and a pulse point beat frantically in the base of her throat. A pulse point he still had an inexplicable urge to cover with his lips. His tongue.

He muttered an old Arabian curse and realised what he'd just done. What was it about this woman that made him unconsciously regress to his native language? *By Allah*... He cursed again. Jerked his eyes back to hers. 'What this is about,' he began with a calmness that belied the heated blood pounding through his veins, 'is that it looks very much like you had my child and didn't tell me.'

If possible, the line between her brows deepened and he had the stupidest notion to place the pad of his finger against it and smooth it away. 'What's her name?' he asked gruffly.

Emerald eyes darkened almost to black before dropping from his. 'This is pointless, Nadir.' Her soft, desperate plea fell between them as insignificant as one of her gauzy dance costumes and he savoured the defeat in it.

'Pointless for you, perhaps,' he agreed pleasantly.

A soft moan broke from her lips and his body registered it as one she used to make in bed and it appalled him that he could be so angry one minute and so aroused the next. It was those damned memories of having her spread out naked on his bed that were the problem.

During his more unguarded moments those memories crept up on him like the flu and reminded him that once—once—he had thought he'd found something special with a woman.

A low growl filled the base of his throat. This, he would have said, was not an unguarded moment and yet his control over his body felt tenuous, tangled up in the silken awareness of the female in front of him, who was dressed in nothing more provocative than denim jeans and a red T-shirt.

'Please, Nadir...'

'Please what, Imogen?' he rasped, hating the sound of his name on her treacherous lips and welcoming another shot of anger as it jetted through him. 'Please forgive you for keeping the birth of my child from me? Because she is mine, isn't she?'

He didn't know if it was his words or his tone

that brought her chin up but her beautiful eyes glittered angrily. 'I did not keep her birth from you. You knew I was pregnant and you didn't want anything to do with her.'

Her voice had grown shrill and a couple of shoppers hesitated before passing them by.

'I don't think so. Now come.'

'You didn't even believe it was your baby. God,' she exclaimed, 'can't you just forget that we ever saw each other again?'

'Like you want to?'

She didn't answer, to her credit, which was just as well because his control was heading in the same direction as his day. 'Tell me,' he began silkily. 'Do you believe in fate, Imogen?'

'No.'

'Then you'll just have to put this meeting down to luck, won't you?'

She glared at him and pulled her bottom lip between her teeth, which meant she was thinking hard. Not that it mattered. He stepped closer to her, inhaling her wonderful, sweet scent that was somehow the same and yet different. He swallowed against a sudden rush of conscience. He had nothing to feel guilty about here. 'You're coming with me,' he said quietly. 'Even if I have to put you into that car myself.'

Her brows shot up at that. 'Not even you would do something so heinous.'

Nadir gave a sharp bark of laughter. If only she knew how close he was to doing *exactly* that.

'Then what are you afraid of, *habibi*?'

'I'm not afraid. I'm confused,' she said with bald honesty. 'What do you want?'

'To talk.' He had a lot of questions to clear up; not least of all was how she had hidden herself away so effectively his security team hadn't been able to find her until now. And then there was the small matter that he wanted to be a part of his child's life. A permanent part. But he had no doubt she'd welcome that. It would mean money and status and he hadn't met many people who wouldn't put that ahead of integrity and self-respect.

CHAPTER THREE

IMOGEN SLICKED HER tongue across her dry lips, her heart pounding towards a heart attack as Nadir led her towards the car.

To talk, he said. But was that really what he wanted? And why was he so angry with her about Nadeena?

Every instinct in her body warned her that she shouldn't go with him but really she wasn't afraid of Nadir. And, despite his hostile manner, it wasn't as if he would want to have anything to do with Nadeena in the long run.

In truth, he probably just wanted to make sure she wasn't going to go to the press with news of his indiscretion. Her stomach turned. That was the most likely scenario here. That and to en-sure that she wasn't going to make any financial demands on him in the future. Maybe he'd even offer to set up a trust fund for Nadeena. If he did, she wouldn't take it. She would provide for her daughter herself. Nadeena need never know that her father hadn't loved her enough to want her in his life.

Unable to stop herself, her eyes ran over his face. He was still the most ruggedly attractive man she had ever laid eyes on, with thick black hair that fell in long layers, olive skin and an aquiline nose that perfectly offset a square jaw that always looked as if it was in need of a shave. And his mouth. Surely that had been fashioned by Ishtar because it could look either surly or sexy depending on his mood.

Currently, he wasn't in a good one. But okay, she would be rational. Talk to him. Answer his banal questions. Reassure him that she wanted nothing from him. 'Fine. I can give you a few minutes.'

He didn't answer and warning bells clanged loudly inside her head again as the car door was smoothly opened by a burly chauffer. Then a waft of deliciously cool air hit her and she bent her head and manoeuvred inside as best she could with Nadeena still strapped to her chest.

'Wouldn't you be better taking that thing off?'

His gruff question came from the opposite seat and Imogen momentarily lost her train of thought as his masculine scent enveloped her. 'That *thing* is a sling and no, I can't. Not without waking her.'

'So wake her.'

'Not a good idea. Don't you know you should never wake a sleeping baby?'

His slight hesitation was loaded. 'How would I?'

Cold censure laced every word and she had to force her eyes to remain connected to his. Nadeena really did have his eyes, she thought absurdly. Lucky her. 'So I'm here.' She let out a pent-up breath. 'So talk.'

'This is not a conversation for a limousine.' Nadir made a motion with his hand and said something in rapid-fire...Italian? Greek? Before Imogen knew it, the car was in motion.

'Wait. Where are we going?'

Nadir's eyes snagged with hers and the heat from his gaze made her go still all over. His eyes drifted over her face with insolent slowness and sexual awareness turned her mouth as dry as dust.

Determined not to be so weakened by him again that she turned into a puppet on a string, she forced air in and out of her lungs in a steady stream. But the act took up every ounce of her concentration so when he informed her that they were going to his apartment it took longer than it should have for his words to take hold.

'Your apartment? No.' She shook her head. 'You've misunderstood me. I meant a few minutes *here*. In the car. And it's illegal to drive with an infant not strapped into a proper baby carrier.'

Nadir leaned forward and spoke to his driver again and instantly the big car slowed.

'My apartment is close by. And it is you who has misunderstood me, Imogen. We have to talk and a few minutes isn't even going to cover the first topic.'

Imogen narrowed her eyes. 'I don't see why. I did what you wanted fourteen months ago and disappeared from your sight so I don't understand what you want with me now.'

His sculptured lips thinned into a grim line. 'You did disappear, I'll give you that. And you still haven't told me her name.'

Her name? Imogen lowered her gaze to the safety of her daughter's head. No way could she reveal her name. No way did she want to see this man who had once meant so much to her mock her for her sentimentality. Maybe even pity her. At the time she'd named her she'd been feeling particularly sorry for herself and hopelessly alone. The three-day blues they called the come down from the emotional high some women experienced after giving birth. Now she wished she'd named her Meredith or Jessica—or any name other than the one she had.

Fortunately the car pulled up at the kerb before she had to answer and, feeling sick, she followed Nadir as he strode through the large foyer of his building with a bronzed water feature at one end and a smartly dressed concierge at the other.

'When did you move to London?' she asked, suddenly wondering if they had been living in the same city the whole time.

'I didn't.' He stabbed at the button to call the lift and she remembered that of course he had apartments in most of the major financial centres in the world.

Casting a quick glance around his beautifully appointed living room, she inwardly shook her head at the absurd difference in their lifestyles. Of course she'd known that he was wealthy when she'd met him—her fellow dancers had informed her as to whom he was—but, apart from his outrageously divine apartment on the Île Saint-Louis, their time together had been incredibly normal.

Nights in bed, mornings at the local patisserie, afternoons strolling or jogging along the Seine. More time in bed.

Shaking off the rush of memories, she headed straight for a set of plush sofas and laid Nadeena on one. Glancing back at Nadir, she asked him to hand her the baby bag he'd carried up and checked Nadeena's nappy while he stood beside her.

Of course Nadeena went quiet in that moment. Her big, curious eyes riveted to Nadir, as most other females were when they first clapped eyes on him. She blinked as if trying to clear her vision and a small frown formed between her round silvery-blue eyes.

'She has my eyes,' he said hoarsely.

The sense of awe in his voice was hard to miss and an unexpected swell of emotions surged inside Imogen's chest. Emotions that were so twisted together they were too difficult to define.

'Here you go, little one.' She lifted Nadeena into her arms and settled her back in the crook of her shoulder, silently willing her not to complain. Then she glanced at Nadir. 'I need to feed her.'

Nadir waved his hand negligently. 'Go ahead.'

Imogen moistened her lips. 'I'd like some privacy.'

He paused and Imogen was sure her cheeks turned scarlet.

'You breastfeed?'

Even though she had breastfed in cafés and parks and not blinked an eye before, this moment, in a quiet living room with a man she had once believed she had fallen in love with felt far too intimate. His continued perusal sent another frisson of unwelcome awareness zipping through her. 'Yes.'

She knew her voice sounded husky and when her eyes met his she couldn't hold his stare. What was she doing here in this room with him? More importantly, what was he doing in this room with her and Nadeena? She felt self-conscious and it was all too easy to remember how it felt to have him at her breast, drawing her aching nipple deep into his mouth. All too easy to recall the pleasure that had turned her into an incoherent puppet for him to master at his will.

When she continued to hesitate and Nadeena grew restless Nadir pivoted on his foot and stalked to the long windows overlooking some sort of dense green park that most likely belonged to him as well. Imogen quickly arranged her T-shirt and

Nadeena latched on like a baby that had never fed before.

'When were you going to tell me I had fathered a child, Imogen?' His quiet question held a wealth of judgement and loathing behind it and Imogen felt as if someone had just dropped an icy blanket around her shoulders.

She didn't look at him. She couldn't because all of a sudden she felt horribly guilty about the fact that she had never intended to tell him. And hot on the heels of her unexpected guilt rode anger. Anger she welcomed with open arms. *He* was the one who had run away when he'd learned she was pregnant, not *her*. *He* was the one who had made it clear that he didn't want a baby in his life when she had felt such a rush of elation at the time she had almost grinned at him like a loon. Then she'd seen his stricken face and her world had fallen apart.

A sound like a low growl came from deep in Nadir's throat and he towered over her. 'Never? Is that the word that is at this moment stuck in your throat, *habibi*?'

'Don't call me that,' Imogen growled back, unable to contain her rioting emotions.

'It's preferable to what I want to call you, believe me.'

Imogen had never seen Nadir angry before and he was magnificent with it. Fierce and proud and so *powerful*.

She swallowed, hating that she still found him so utterly attractive. 'How dare you come over like the injured party in this scenario?' she snapped. She was the one who had been as sick as a dog carrying Nadeena. She was the one who had been all alone in the birthing suite as Nadeena had come into the world. She was the one who struggled day to day with the demands of motherhood and putting food in their mouths. And she had asked for nothing from him. Absolutely nothing. 'I have done very well for myself since you left my life,' she said, her body vibrating with tension. 'I have survived very well on my own. I've eked out a life for myself and Nadeena is healthy. She's happy and—'

'Nadeena?'

Imogen's eyes squeezed shut and her temper deflated when he repeated the baby's name. His irreverent tone somehow made her remember how lonely she had felt when Nadir had walked away from her. She'd felt lonely before, of course, but with Nadir she had felt as if she had got a glimpse—a *taste*—of paradise, only to have it snatched away when she was least prepared.

Powerful memories surged again and she couldn't look at him. 'Why am I here, Nadir?'

He didn't say anything, his eyes troubled as they made contact with her own. He leant against the cherry wood dining table, his gaze riveted to Nadeena, kneading her T-shirt like a contented cat, his silence drawing out the moment. Drawing out her nerves until they lay just beneath the fine layer of her skin like freshly tuned guitar strings. 'Why is there no public record of her birth?'

Bewildered by both the flat tenor of his voice and the unexpected question, Imogen frowned. 'There is.'

His gaze sharpened and she could see his agile mind turning. 'Under what name?'

Imogen stared at him. At the time of Nadeena's birth she had only put her own name down on the birth certificate. She hadn't known what to put in place of the father's and a kindly registrar had told her that it wasn't essential information. That she could fill that part out later. So far, that section was still blank because she'd been so busy and so tired learning how to care for an infant she hadn't even thought about putting Nadir's name on it. Sensing that this was a loaded question, she raised her chin. 'Mine.'

'Imogen Reid.'

His earlier words—*I have not searched for you for the past fourteen months to be given the run-around now'*—and his personal bodyguard waiting for his arrival came back to her and clicked into place in her mind and confused her even more. 'Benson.'

There was only the briefest of pauses before he roared, 'You gave me a false name!'

Imogen pressed back against the seat of the sofa. 'No.' Well, not intentionally. 'Reid was my mother's maiden name and...' She swallowed, hating herself for explaining but compelled to do so by the fury she read in his eyes. 'It wasn't deliberate. The girls suggested that I use a stage name because they sometimes had trouble with the clientele and you only asked me my name one time.' She took a quick breath. 'At the beginning.'

He stabbed a hand through his hair and paced across the room like an animal trapped in a too-narrow cage. 'And your mobile phone number?'

'What about it?'

'You changed it.'

'I lost it…well, it was stolen my first day in London. I just use a pay-as-you-go now.'

He swore under his breath, a ferocious sound.

'What's this about, Nadir? As I recall you were the one who left town the morning after you found out I was pregnant. Are you now saying you tried to contact me?' She tried to stifle a small thrill inside, wondering if perhaps he had been worried about her. That perhaps he had cared for her after all… Another more skeptical voice reminded her of the horrible text he'd sent her but still some deeply buried hope wriggled its way to the surface.

'I had an emergency in New York and by the time I got back to Paris you had disappeared as if you'd never existed,' Nadir grated. 'The Ottoman Empire would have benefited from your stealth.'

Resenting his sarcasm, she stiffened. 'I did not disappear. I left.'

'Without a trace. No one had any idea where you had gone.'

That was most likely because the only person who knew had been Minh's sister, Caro, and she had been leaving to go travelling at the same time. Imogen had meant to keep in touch with some of the other girls but she hadn't counted on feeling sick and sorry for herself during her pregnancy and she hadn't had time since then.

'Nor did you give your employer a forwarding address or email.'

'I didn't?' She blinked. 'I wasn't exactly thinking straight at the time.' And since her pay went directly into her bank account, she hadn't even realised. 'I'm surprised you didn't check my bank records.'

His look said that he had. 'False names tend to hinder that kind of search.'

'I told you that wasn't deliberate.' She took a deep breath and tried to keep a lid on her emotions so she could think rationally. 'Why were you looking for me, anyway?'

'Because before you ran you were supposedly pregnant with my child.'

'I did not *run*,' she bit out tensely. 'Why would I when you had made it abundantly clear you didn't want anything to do with me any more?'

She heard the challenge in her voice and knew it was because some part of her was hoping he would refute her statement.

'I texted you from New York.'

Her top lip curled with distaste. That horrible

text was still etched into her brain as if it had been carved there. 'Oh, please,' she scoffed, 'let's not talk about your lovely text.'

'Or your response,' he grated. 'Telling me that you had *taken care of everything.*'

Imogen tossed her ponytail over her shoulder, careful not to awaken Nadeena, who had dropped into another exhausted sleep. 'I did take care of it,' she said softly, her arms tightening around Nadeena.

'Yes, but not in the way I expected.'

Hoped, his tone seemed to imply. And there was the reason he'd been looking for her. He'd wanted to make sure she'd done what he expected.

Imogen felt that small spark of hope that she'd been wrong about him completely wither and die and she felt angry with herself for succumbing to it in the first place. Had she not learned anything from his treatment of her in the past?

Caro's words of warning came back to her. *'Be careful, Imogen. Any man who takes off like that without a word and accuses you of sleeping around is likely to insist on an abortion if he ever comes back.'* At the time Imogen had thought her friend had been overreacting. Now she knew that she hadn't been and she felt physically ill.

'And now you'll have to deal with the consequences,' he grated, staring at her as if she was somehow to blame for everything that was wrong in the world.

CHAPTER FOUR

IMOGEN LAPSED INTO a horrified silence, focusing on her daughter instead of the sick feeling swirling in the pit of her stomach.

Quite honestly she had never expected to see Nadir again and she really wished she hadn't. But at least he'd well and truly put paid to those times she'd wondered if she shouldn't contact him and let him know that his child had been born. Put paid to those silly girlish fantasies that he would one day ride in on a big white horse and offer her undying love.

Yeah, right. Probably she'd listened to way too many love songs while she had been incapacitated on Minh's sofa and possibly watched way too much day time TV.

But at least that whole time hadn't been a complete waste. She'd used it to plan out her and her baby's future and decided to follow a long-held dream and teach dance. She'd even taken a short online business course. She had a vision that when she had enough money she and Nadeena would move to a mid-sized town where she could open a studio. Nadeena would rush home after school and if she wanted to she could dance; if not, she could sit and do homework or read. Then they would go home together and chat while Imogen cooked dinner and at night...at night...she hadn't really thought about the nights. Her imagination had only gone so far as to envision her and Nadeena as a tight-knit unit.

The two of them happy and contented.

And when Nadeena asked about her father, as she surely would one day, Imogen hadn't quite worked out what she was going to tell her. She didn't want to lie to her but nor did she want Nadeena to know that her father had never wanted her. She glanced at Nadir standing by the window, his broad back to her as if he couldn't stand to look at her. Well, that was fine with her. She couldn't stand to look at him either.

Careful not to waken Nadeena, she eased herself off the sofa, not as easy as it looked since it was one of those squishy ones designed for long afternoons lazing about, and cradled Nadeena in her arms.

Hearing her, Nadir turned towards her and she hastily pulled her T-shirt back into place.

'Where do you think you're going?'

Imogen raised her chin at his surly tone. 'Home.'

'To that buffoon you were with earlier?'

It took her a beat to realise he was referring to Minh but she wasn't about to get into another lengthy discussion with him and, although it was illogical, her gut warned her that if she answered his question honestly he'd never let her leave. And that was exactly what she was about to do. 'You have no right to ask me that. But I am curious as to why you brought me up here. It seems like a waste of your time and mine.'

His eyes held hers and he continued as if she hadn't spoken. 'Is he your current lover?'

Chilled, Imogen cuddled Nadeena closer. 'You answer my questions and I'll answer yours.'

'I'm sorry.' Nadir's voice, his stance—heck, his very demeanour—had turned alert with predatory intent. 'Did you assume you were in a position to bargain with me?'

Imogen rubbed the space between her eyes, her arms starting to ache from holding Nadeena.

'What I assumed,' she said as she laid her daughter on the sofa and fixed cushions around her, 'was that you weren't interested in anything about me and what I do, or where I live.'

'You are the mother of my child,' he said as if that answered everything.

And then she remembered why she was here and could have laughed at her own stupidity. This wasn't about some romantic reunion of past lovers. This was about a man with self-preservation on his mind. 'We've already established that you don't care about that.'

'I care.'

Imogen curled her lip. What he meant was that he cared about how much cash she was going to hit him up for.

'I get it,' she said tonelessly. 'And while I think it's incredibly selfish of you not to want to provide for your own flesh and blood you'll no doubt be relieved to know that I don't want anything from you and I never will.'

'Excuse me?'

'Nor do I expect that you will want to see her and that's more than okay with me as well.'

He started to laugh and she felt even more disgusted with him. 'I don't see what's so amusing. It's a travesty if you really think about it too much. Which I try not to do.'

'You're serious.'

'I certainly don't think abandoning your own child is something to laugh about, but maybe that's just me.'

'Except I didn't abandon her—you took her.'

'Are we back to that again?'

His eyebrow rose. 'Did we ever leave it?'

'I want to go home, Nadir.'

'That's not possible,' he said briskly. 'I should have already left for Bakaan by now.'

His homeland?

'Please don't let me stop you.'

One corner of his mouth quirked in a parody of a smile. 'I don't intend to. But unfortunately we have run out of time to get things you might need from your house. If you write me a list I'll make sure you have everything on hand when we arrive. We shouldn't be gone long. A day at the most.'

Imogen blinked. 'We?'

'That's what I said.'

'You must be mad.'

He pulled his phone out of his pocket and started dialling as if he hadn't heard her.

'Nadir, what are you doing?'

He looked up at her. 'Claiming what is mine.'

Imogen waited a beat before responding. Waited

for the punchline. When he stared back with all the confidence of a man used to getting his own way she felt dizzy.

'I am not yours and I never was!'

He raised an eyebrow. 'I meant Nadeena.'

Sanctimonious bastard.

Embarrassed at her gaffe, Imogen hauled the baby bag over her shoulder. 'Didn't you just hear me? I said I don't want anything from you.'

'I heard you.'

She shook her head. 'I'm going.'

Before she had time to reach Nadeena, Nadir abandoned his call and yanked the bag off her shoulder, spinning her around to face him. 'You've stolen the first five months of my daughter's life from me.' His voice seemed to harden with every word even though its tenor didn't change. 'You won't be stealing any more.'

Stolen? Imogen's knees started to shake and the sense of dread from earlier returned with force. 'I haven't stolen anything. And how do you know she's even really yours?'

A grim smile crooked the corner of his mouth. 'She has my eyes.'

'Lots of people have silvery-blue eyes,' she said on a rush. 'They're as common as mice.' Rats.

One dark eyebrow rose. 'You gave her an Arabic name.'

'Nadeena was a great-aunt of mine.'

'And you're proving to be a terrible liar. Which is in your favour.'

'I don't understand this at all.' She threw her arms up in front of her. 'You don't even want children. Why would you want us to go with you?'

He widened his stance and her eyes couldn't help but notice his strong legs and lean torso. God, did he have to be quite so damned virile?

'How do you know that?'

Gossip, mainly. She lifted her chin and focused on his hard face, which wasn't much better. 'Well, do you?' she asked coolly.

'I'd say that's a moot point now, wouldn't you?'

'No, I most definitely would not. I'd say it's very relevant considering the way you're behaving.'

'Sometimes, Imogen, life throws us curve balls but that doesn't mean we have to drop them. I don't need a DNA test to confirm that I have a child.'

Frustration made her voice sharper than usual. 'Of course you need to do a DNA test. What kind of crazy talk is that? No rich man in his right mind would take on a child as his own without doing a DNA test.'

Nadir laughed and this time it rang with genuine amusement. 'You always were just that little bit different from the pack, *habibi.*' His voice, so gentle and deep, brought a rush of memories back into her dizzy brain. 'But you need not worry. I plan to do my duty by her.'

His duty?

A sense of terror entered her heart. Was that what he meant by saying he'd be claiming what was his? She didn't want to know. Not right now. 'I don't need you to do the right thing by Nadeena.' She'd been looking out for herself for a long time now and she could look out for her child as well.

Nadir raked an impatient hand through his hair. 'Nevertheless, I will.' His striking eyes narrowed. 'Now quit arguing and give me a list of things you will need for our flight to Bakaan.'

Striving for calm, Imogen tried to slow down her heart that was banging away inside her chest so loudly he must surely be able to hear it. Right now she felt as if she was trying to survive a fierce gale that was corralling her towards the edge of a very high cliff. Then a horrible thought froze the blood inside her veins. 'I won't let you take my baby, Nadir.' She hated that her voice rang with fear. 'If that's your plan.' She'd never even considered it before but now that she had she couldn't push it from her mind.

He glanced at her impatiently. 'If I wanted that then you couldn't stop me.'

'I could. I'd…' Panic clawed inside her throat. 'I'll…'

'But I don't want that.' He made an impatient gesture with his hands. 'I am not so callous that I don't realise that a baby needs its mother. That is why I plan to marry you.'

Marry her!

She shook her head, biting back a rising sense of hysteria. She needed time to make sense of everything that was happening and she couldn't because her mind didn't know which way to turn.

'Breathe, Imogen.' Nadir went to put his hands on her shoulders and she jerked back, wondering how he had got so close to her without her being aware of it.

Imogen shook her head, fear spiking inside her like a flash of lightning. 'You're crazy to think that I'd marry you after the way you treated me.'

Nadir's mouth thinned and he stepped closer to

her, contained anger emanating from every taut line of his body. 'I can assure you that I'm not. I've had a lot of time to review my options while you were in hiding and this is non-negotiable.'

Imogen tried to still the trembling inside her body. 'I was not hiding.'

'It's irrelevant now.'

She laughed. What else could she do? 'You can't just come back into my life and think you can do whatever you want.' Her father had behaved that way. Coming and going as he pleased with little concern for either her or her mother. As if she'd shackle her and her daughter to a man cut from the same cloth. 'I'll fight you.'

'What with?' She hadn't realised that her hands had balled into tight white fists until Nadir's mocking gaze drew hers to them. He reached out and raised them in front of her, enclosing them inside his much larger grip. 'With these, hmm? I have to confess that, as aggressive as you can be in bed, I didn't take you for the violent type.'

She wouldn't have before today either. 'Nadir, we had an affair,' she cried, throwing his earlier words back in his face and tugging at his implacable hold. 'We only had sex a…a…a couple of times.'

He resisted her feeble attempts to break free with embarrassing ease and hauled her closer. 'Let's see,' he said with a snarl. 'Four weekends, around three times a day, more at night.' His eyes dropped to her mouth and lingered before returning to hers. 'You don't have to be Einstein to know that comes to more than *a couple of times, habibi*. And it was good sex.'

His words and his tone combined to set off a wildfire reaction inside her body.

'It meant nothing,' she choked out, still trying to free her hands from within the prison of his. Wishing that his grip was hurting her to distract her from the riot of sensations being this close to him was setting off inside her. She couldn't seem to focus her thoughts when she became enshrouded in his earthy male scent, the sensitive tips of her breasts rising against the lace of her bra and the deep achy feeling between her thighs reminding her of how it had once been between them.

'Nothing?' His soft question had a lethal undertone that had her raising her eyes to his, but she only reached his mouth, which seemed so close to her own that if she held still long enough she was sure she could feel his breath against her lips. 'Nothing, Imogen? I don't think so.'

'I'll get a lawyer,' she said breathlessly, yanking harder on her hands, only to find that they were now trapped against his hard chest.

He laughed. 'From what I know of your finances, you can't afford a decent babysitter.'

'Bastard!'

His eyes bored holes into hers. 'And what court of law is going to side with a mother who kept a child's existence from its father? Who leaves her baby with friends while she works?'

'Lots of mothers do that.'

'Yes, but lots of mothers do not have a child of royal blood. Nadeena is a Bakaani princess.'

'I don't think of her like that.'

'Right.'

'I don't!' she exclaimed at his cynical tone. 'She's just an innocent baby to me, not a commodity. And no court in the world would favour a father who thinks like that.'

Nadir arched a brow. 'You're not that naïve, surely.'

'Nadir, stop this, I beg you.'

'Do you?'

She flushed, remembering the last time she'd

said those words to him. It might as well have been five minutes ago for the response of her body. The feeling of being helpless beneath him, her hands held above her head as he'd nudged her thighs wider with his knees, the feel of his silken hardness at that first moment he pushed himself inside her body, that feeling of her softness giving way to all that male strength in inexorable pleasure.

Her body clenched and mortification filled her. She tried to twist away from him now but somehow that only made her more aware of the press of his hips, forcing the hard ridge of his erection into her belly.

Erection!

Imogen's eyes flew to his. 'No.'

He gave a hollow laugh. 'Oh, yes, Imogen, you still turn me on,' he said thickly. 'Despite your treachery.'

His head descended towards hers and she shoved against his chest. She didn't want him—not again. He'd accused her of sleeping with someone else while seeing him—had probably done so himself while he was seeing her—he'd thought they were having an affair that he'd had no trouble ending while she had nearly died inside when he'd walked away from her. She didn't want him. She couldn't!

But she did and none of that mattered to her wounded heart when his lips touched hers in a searing kiss that narrowed the time they had been apart to nothing. Still, she attempted to resist him, clamping her lips into a straight line that, in the end, was no defence at all.

Certainly no defence against her own raging need to touch him and be touched by him and when he took advantage of her confusion and drove his tongue into her mouth Imogen was lost. He just felt too good, tasted too good, and it had been so long for her. So long since she had felt the press of a man's lips. The press of *his* lips.

All of a sudden she was no longer pushing him away, but drawing him closer. Her hands flattening over the hard muscles of his chest to snake up around his neck, her mouth moving beneath his in an age-old request for more. And he gave it to her. Eagerly. Impatiently. Thrusting his tongue into her mouth and drinking in her very essence.

His other hand came up to cup her jaw, holding her steady. A low groan, more like the growl of a hungry wolf, worked its way out of his throat as he angled his mouth over hers and ravaged her lips as if he was as desperate for her as she was for him.

Nothing else seemed to matter in that moment. The room disappeared. The world. It was just the two of them. As it always had been when they'd come together. Like magic.

'Nadir,' she whispered, shuddering against him as his strong fingers followed the line of her spine, spanning her waist before dropping lower to cup her bottom and bring her even closer. Unbearably close. Imogen squirmed and forked her hands into his hair to anchor herself to him, one leg already rising to rest over his lean hip.

And then suddenly she was free and he had stepped back from her, reaching out to steady her as she stumbled without his body weight to hold her up. 'It seems I still turn you on as well, hmm, *habibi*?'

What?

Dazed, she blinked up at him and then his condescending words hit her and she was instantly appalled at her behaviour.

Had he just kissed her to prove a point? To prove how weak she was when it came to him? To prove how much power he still had over her? Her face flamed and she was so angry she wanted to punch him.

Realising just how close she was to hitting someone for the first time in her life, she lowered her bunched fists to her sides. 'Don't ever touch me again.' *Was she hyperventilating?* She placed a hand against her chest. It felt as if she was hyperventilating. 'I hate you, Nadir. I *really* hate you.'

'Don't be stupid about this, Imogen,' he rasped, pulling his phone from his pocket again. 'You can't provide everything our daughter needs and I want her to grow up secure.'

'I want that too. Which is why I would *never* marry you.'

From the stiffening of his spine she could see that he didn't like that. 'Be serious,' she continued desperately, trying to appeal to his rational side. 'You never *wanted* Nadeena.'

'I may not have *planned* Nadeena.' His expression grew fierce. 'But she is here and this is the best solution.'

Imogen's nostrils flared as if she was a lioness sensing danger. Nadeena's emotional welfare was on the line and Imogen had vowed a long time ago that she would rather be a single mother than have her child raised by a parent who didn't want her. Especially the autocratic tyrant Nadir had turned into. But then maybe he had always been that way. She had never challenged him before, had she? 'This is the *worst* solution.'

Nadir put the phone to his ear. 'Bjorn, tell Vince we'll be at the airport within the hour.'

He rang off and Imogen felt icy-cold with dread. 'You selfish bastard,' she raged raggedly. 'You won't even consider my needs.'

'Actually, I would say I was considering them very well.'

'Ha!' she scorned. 'You're nothing but a bully.'

His eyes flashed a warning she was in no mood to heed. 'Careful, Imogen. I will only tolerate so much from you.'

'Like I care,' she fumed, restless energy making her muscles vibrate. 'You can't do this, you know. I have rights.'

She stared at him as if she really knew what she was talking about but inside she was quaking. Not that she'd let him see that. The stakes were far too high for him to think that he had the upper hand. For him to assume that she was a pushover.

'What you have,' he said in a carefully modulated tone, his face a cold mask, 'is my child.'

A discreet knock at the door interrupted the stark silence that followed that statement and Nadir turned to answer it.

'And Imogen?' She glanced at him, hoping he was about to tell her this had all been a joke. 'You *will* marry me.'

It was a great parting shot, she thought as she sagged against the arm of the sofa and speared wishful daggers into his broad back. But she would have the last word because she would never marry a man she didn't love.

CHAPTER FIVE

THE PLANE TOOK off into the air and Nadir wondered if he needed to have his head examined for bringing Imogen and Nadeena to Bakaan with him.

He could have easily had Bjorn or any one of his men watch her. And what was with the announcement that he was going to marry her?

He scowled. He hadn't intended to blurt it out like that but hell, that woman could make him do things he'd never intended to do. She always could.

Back in Paris it had been her coy smiles to get him to play tourist or to laze around reading the Sunday papers over brunch. Who had time for that, anyway? Not him. And the fact that he'd done it still rankled.

He'd been so overcome with lust back then he'd let her call the shots. He wouldn't do that again. Not that he was planning to be an asshole about it. He wasn't. But nor was he going to be hood-winked by her nice girl persona either. Hood-winked by her innocent sexuality.

No. She'd run once. He wouldn't give her the chance to do it again.

Still, he could have waited until he returned to-morrow afternoon before revealing his plan and he had no ready answer as to why he hadn't.

Probably he'd still been shocked from finding her with his child. That had to be it. He gulped down a mouthful of water from the bottle his staff had handed him upon boarding. He noticed that Imogen hadn't accepted one and he frowned.

She hadn't said boo to him since they'd left his apartment and that was fine with him. All except for the way she made him feel that she was being some sort of martyr in coming with him. And why would she be?

It didn't make sense. Was she still playing him in some way? Acting hard to get to whet his ap-petite? Not that it had worked. That kiss… He scrubbed a hand across his face, gulped down more water. He hadn't meant to kiss her before, let alone back her against the wall. And he didn't like to admit that he'd got lost in that kiss. Only the fact that she had as well had salved his pride.

Damn, but she tasted sweet. Exactly as he'd re-membered. Even now his body throbbed with an inexplicable urge to have her. It was like a driv-ing need. All-consuming. It had always bothered him. The extent of his need. Needing people led to emotional weakness, which led to mistakes being made. He knew that better than anyone and yet fifteen months ago he'd let himself be drawn into her silken web anyway.

Of its own accord, his mind returned to the Sun-day afternoon he had found out she was preg-nant—an extraordinary blue-sky summer day in Paris. Not wanting to think about his later flight home to New York, they had wandered around Paname—as the Parisians affectionately called their city. He had shown Imogen some of his fa-vourite haunts and she'd dragged him around what felt like every flea market in the known universe. That was where he'd learned she adored Auber-gine Provençal and that she was a hoarder of an-cient postcards and scarves. The afternoon had ended with her vomiting over his toilet bowl and a doctor announcing her condition with a happy flourish that had floored him.

And okay, he hadn't taken the news that well. What contented bachelor would? So he'd flown back to New York and called his thousand-dollar-an-hour lawyer.

'First, establish the kid is yours.'

When Nadir had told him that was going to be a nine-month wait, his lawyer had shaken his head. 'Not so,' he'd said. 'Modern medicine has moved right along. There's a test, see. It's called some amnio thing. I had to arrange one for a client a few months back. Boy, was he relieved when the results came back negative. The lady had been sleeping around. Tried to pin him with someone else's kid.'

His lawyer had *tsk*ed in disgust and Nadir had murmured some agreement. Asking Imogen to take the test had made sense. So he'd texted her with the request. Perfectly reasonable in his view.

Finding her gone without a trace when he'd flown back to Paris hadn't been reasonable at all.

A dream he'd often had over the last fourteen months winged into his consciousness. It had always been about a child of indiscriminate gender. But the eyes had always been emerald-green and ringed with brown curly lashes. Usually the baby then became the woman, which was when he usually woke up. Usually sweating. Usually cursing.

* * *

He thought about her claim that she hadn't run away from him. The different surname. His gut tightened. Was he being played for a fool? And what was up with the buffoon who had tried to defend her? The one who had trod off like a trained seal at her bidding.

Seeing Imogen with her arm linked through his, that sweet smile on her face that could fell an army of warriors…another screw in his gut turned.

She lived with him. He knew that and the water turned sour in his mouth. He'd nearly decked the guy when he'd tried to keep him from her. As if he'd had a chance. On some level he knew his reaction wasn't logical, but logic had never been his firm friend when she was around.

He glanced over as she laughed at something Nadeena had done. He had always loved her laugh. Deep and throaty and redolent of all the pent-up passion of her personality. She had laughed a lot when they had been together. Laughed and teased him as no one else ever had. And she had done it right away, something he'd found as sexy as hell. As sexy as he found her now in faded denims and a simple cotton T-shirt. As sexy as he found her—

Breathing? a mocking voice in his head suggested.

No, Nadir silently snarled back.

And why was he even thinking like this? Brooding over things he couldn't change wouldn't make this whole situation any easier. It didn't matter that he had never met a woman who affected him as strongly—or as quickly—as Imogen. It didn't matter that she made him angry or frustrated or horny or hell—guilty. What mattered was that they get married and make the best of the situation.

What mattered was that he was a father.

A father.

Hell. The thought rocked him. But he knew it was true. He had known the minute the kid had looked up at him with his twin sister's soulful eyes staring back at him. His eyes. And Imogen had given her an Arabic name as if she'd been racked with guilt over knowing she was never going to tell him about his child. Anger rolled through his blood, thick and renewed, and he recalled how she'd called him a bully. Did she just expect him to give up on his daughter without a fight? Whether she liked it or not, he had a hundred options up his sleeve. And he didn't give a damn how Imogen felt about that because he wanted his daughter.

He had wanted Nadeena—truly wanted her— from the moment he had looked at her with her chubby hands fisted on Imogen's soft breast and her wide eyes staring up at him as if she was trying to learn everything about him, as if she was looking directly into his soul. He swallowed heavily. He'd taken one look at her and he'd been... he'd been smitten.

It had been the same the first time he had looked at Imogen and felt that his life would never be the same again.

Hell. What was he thinking?

His life hadn't changed when he'd first laid eyes on Imogen. They had only been having an affair.

No, his life had changed when she had become pregnant with his baby. And now hers was about to change and he had no doubt that she would acquiesce when she got down from her high horse and realised how much he could provide for her. He nearly laughed. As if she hadn't already thought of that.

But that was okay. He could live with her wanting him for his money. It would be a small price to pay to know that his daughter was safe and well.

He signalled the hostess waiting to serve them. This was going to be okay.

'Yes, sir.'

'Coffee, please and...' he glanced at Imogen '...food for Miss Reid—Benson. I haven't noticed her eating anything yet.'

'Miss Benson said she's not hungry, sir.'

Nadir checked out the thin outline of her once curvy body. 'Give her something anyway. Have the chef cook up Aubergine Provençal.'

'I'm sorry, sir. What was that?'

Yeah, what was *that?* He scowled. 'An omelette, then. Something. Anything. Just as long as it's vegetarian.'

'Of course, sir.'

Nadir flipped open his laptop, determined to focus on work for the rest of the trip. Once he renounced the throne tomorrow and married Imogen his life could get back to normal. Or as normal as it would be with a wife and a child and why didn't that notion bother him half as much as it had fourteen months ago?

Marriage?

The word clunked around in Imogen's brain for the millionth time like a giant-sized anvil and she hoped to God Nadir was at this very minute coming to his senses and seeing how ridiculous the idea was.

The best solution...

Of course there were other solutions, and she'd looked some up on her phone as she'd waited for his plane to take off. Not that she wanted to head down the shared custody route and she was sure—once he had calmed down and thought rationally—that neither would he. What rich playboy would? Especially once he learned how detrimental having a child would be to his bachelor lifestyle and she had every intention of pointing it out to him. Because, although she didn't think those things, she knew that once the reality of parenthood set in Nadir would never take his responsibilities seriously. Not with his reputation as a serial dater. No, he wasn't the faithful type and she'd been serious when she'd told him she wouldn't marry him.

And he couldn't force her. No one could do that in this day and age. The worst he could do was to take her to court and fight for custody of Nadeena. And that was... She swallowed heavily, her eyes darting across the aisle to where he was ensconced in work. Could he win? Would a court of law side with his sob story that she had run away with Nadeena?

Not that she had run; she'd simply taken charge of her life. Taken charge without him in it. And he hadn't wanted to be in it. Or at least that was the message she had taken from his acerbic text.

She still remembered with embarrassing clarity the burst of happiness she had felt when it had pinged into her phone. It had sat there for a full five minutes before she had clicked on it and by then her heart had constructed a full-on fairy tale around what it would say. She had imagined that the text would confirm that he'd had time to think about things and he missed her. That he wanted her in his life. That he wanted their baby. In fact the foolishly sentimental organ in her body had imagined every possible thing he could have written except for what he had.

Imogen, there is a DNA test that can be done while the child is in utero. I have organised an appointment for you at a specialist. If the child is mine I will be in contact.

Devastated by his callousness and influenced by Caro's dire warnings, Imogen had left. And really, what had been the alternative? To write back to him and plead? *Are you sure you don't want our baby? Are you sure you don't want me?* She did have *some* pride.

A delicious smell wafted into the cabin and Imogen's stomach growled as a flight attendant stopped beside her.

'The chef has prepared an omelette for you, Miss Benson. It's vegetarian.'

'Oh.' How had the chef known she was vegetarian? 'I'm sorry. I didn't order this.'

'Prince Nadir ordered it for you.'

Imogen glanced across at the man she was trying hard to think about rationally. Objectively. Something that was almost impossible, given his startling demands and that kiss…

Kiss? She felt a blush heat her cheeks. That kiss had shattered her equilibrium. As had her response. Given his hateful, overbearing behaviour, she'd like to have been left cold when he had touched her. She'd like to have been able to say she was over her sexual infatuation for him and was completely unmoved. She'd also like to be able to say there was no poverty or no ugly wars in the world either.

She sighed and rubbed the back of her neck.

It didn't make sense that he could still make her heart jump just by looking at her and her body throb for more with one touch. How could a man who was a veritable stranger and who totally disregarded her needs and desires still affect her so intensely?

He shouldn't be able to. That was the logical answer. Back in Paris, yes. Back then her mother had just died and her absent father had remarried a month later and Imogen had been looking for a change. She'd been looking for excitement and adventure. She'd been looking for passion.

She pulled a rueful face.

Maybe this was just a case of being careful what you wished for.

Because she'd got it, hadn't she. The excitement. The adventure. The *passion*. She'd got it in the form of a man who had awakened a hunger in her she hadn't even realised she'd possessed and who had given her a child. The child she loved. The child she could deal with. The man not so much. Especially not when he kissed her. When he touched her.

So she'd just have to be ready the next time and make sure he didn't get that close. And maybe he wouldn't try and touch her again because, although he had been as aroused as she had been, he hadn't wanted to desire her any more than she did him.

She watched her daughter stacking wooden blocks together on the floor in front of her and tried not to feel so anxious. She had to trust that even now Nadir was reconsidering his outrageous proposition—because surely no one would call 'You *will* marry me' a proposal. That even now he was trying to come up with a way to bow out of it gracefully.

And if he wasn't, well, Imogen had a plan. She would sit down with him over a cup of tea and she would go over all the information she had down-loaded in a calm and rational manner. She'd point out, in the nicest possible way, that if his actions were motivated by some sort of guilt—or attack of conscience—then he could rest easy because she didn't need him in her life and she certainly didn't want to trap him.

She smiled. That word ought to put the fear of God into him. No man wanted to feel trapped, did they?

'Ma'am? Did you want the omelette?'

Yes, yes, she did. She just didn't want to have anything to do with the man who had ordered it for her. But that wasn't the hostess's fault and Imogen smiled up at her. 'Yes. Thank you.'

Her upbeat thoughts lasted right up until they landed and Imogen found herself in a small airport that made Tullamarine look like LAX. For some reason she'd thought Bakaan would be like Dubai—or the pictures she'd seen of Dubai. It wasn't. But, even so, it was immediately apparent from the few people milling around in traditional garments and the warm dry air that smelled faintly of vanilla and spice that she had entered an ancient realm full of mystique and promise. Much like her impression of Nadir had been that first night.

A shudder ran through her as the car raced through the night dark city and headed up an incline that led to an impressive well-lit palace that sat just above the ancient city like a golden mirage. As much as she hated to admit it, she was a little unsettled and a lot intimidated by the formality of the palace and the very real sense that she was the one who was trapped instead of Nadir.

'My Lord, it is so good to see you again.'

Imogen looked past Nadir to where a small white-haired servant in white robes knelt on the polished stone steps of the palace, his sombre tone increasing Imogen's sense of unease.

'Staph—' Nadir pulled the old servant to his feet '—I told you not to do that the other day.'

He'd been here recently?

The servant's mouth quirked but the solemn note didn't leave his voice. 'We are glad of your return, My Lord.'

'I wish I was.' He switched to Arabic then and the old man bowed at her feet and beamed at her, speaking in rapid-fire Bakaani. She smiled hesitantly, wondering what it was that Nadir had just told him.

'My Lord, Mistress Imogen, Princess Nadeena.'

Shocked at the label he had given her, Imogen shook her head. 'I am not his mistress,' she corrected a little more sharply than she'd intended. Had Nadir told him she was?

The little man dropped to his knees again and started spouting effusively in Bakaani but there was no smile this time.

Confused, Imogen shot Nadir a helpless glance and he sighed. 'Staph meant you no discourtesy, Imogen. The word does not mean the same in our country as it does in the West.'

'Oh, well…please tell him to get up. The ground must be really hard on his knees.'

She felt awful and smiled warmly at the man to show him she hadn't meant to hurt his feelings. 'I'm sorry, I—'

'Leave it, Imogen.'

Nadir's face softened as his eyes fell on his daughter, half asleep in her arms. 'Do you want me to take her?'

'No!' Nadir had offered to take her as they had boarded his plane earlier but she hadn't been ready for that. She still wasn't, even though her reluctance made her feel totally selfish. There was just too much unfinished business between them. 'No. I've got her.'

His eyes narrowed but he didn't push and she was grateful. 'Come then. I will show you to our suite.'

Their suite?

She hurried after him.

'I hope you know I'm not sleeping with you!'

Nadir turned halfway up the steps and the servant cast her a worried look.

Shaking his head, Nadir lowered his voice so he wouldn't be overheard. 'Bakaan is a conservative country, Imogen, and Staph does understand some English. Please keep your discussions about our situation private.'

'I just want you to know that I'm not sleeping in the same bed as you in case you need to organise another room for us,' she half whispered.

'There are many bedrooms in the suite we will be using.'

'Well, good.' She felt her cheeks redden when she realised that he'd just confirmed her earlier suspicion that he didn't want to sleep with her any more than she wanted to sleep with him.

Or any more than she wanted to want to sleep with him, she amended to herself. 'At least we're on the same page about that.'

The look he gave her was a mixture of exasperation and something darker that she couldn't define. 'Imogen, I doubt at this point that we're even in the same book, let alone on the same page. But the steps of the Shomar Palace are not the place to discuss it.'

Silently agreeing, Imogen followed him through a wide doorway into an atrium with high coved ceilings and delicate mosaic-covered walls. The champagne marble tiles that lined the floors and the ornate brickwork dated back to what she thought might be the Moorish period, the surrounding artwork and centuries-old statues recording a history that was both dark and wondrous.

'Has Prince Zachim been notified of our arrival?'

'Yes, My Lord. Will you be needing anything else?'

'Not tonight. Thank you, Staph.'

The man nodded. 'I will bid you goodnight then.' His English was stilted but Imogen appreciated the effort. 'And may I say congratulations, My Lady.'

This time Imogen waited for the servant to retreat before questioning Nadir. 'What is he congratulating me for, exactly?'

'Our marriage. This is your room.' He opened one of the doors inside and waited for her to precede him.

Imogen didn't move, incredulous that Nadir would say such a thing when she had not agreed. 'You told him we were getting married after I distinctly told you we wouldn't be?'

'Not exactly.'

'What does "not exactly" mean?'

'It means he believes we are already married.'

Imogen's brows rose to her hairline. 'I hope

you relieved him of that erroneous view,' she said primly.

When he sighed she knew that he hadn't. 'As I said, Bakaan is a conservative nation.'

'You lied to him. That's why he bowed at my feet.'

'I didn't lie. He assumed we were married.'

'And you let him believe it.'

Nadir's eyes flashed his frustration. 'It was better than the alternative.'

'What? That I was your mistress and had your baby out of wedlock?'

A muscle ticked in his jaw. 'You might not care how Nadeena is perceived in the future, but I do.'

'Of course I care. You're just twisting my words to suit yourself but as soon as I see that man again I'm going to correct him.'

'No, you won't. I won't have Nadeena's name smeared because you can't see reason.'

'I can't see reason?' So much for her hope that he would use the time on the plane to reconsider his proposition.

He stopped directly in front of her. 'And, to all intents and purposes, we are married.'

Imogen coughed out a protest. 'We most certainly are not.'

'Signing a piece of paper isn't going to make it any more real, Imogen. You're going to have to get over whatever reservations you have and get used to it. But we can talk about this later, hmm? It is not a conversation we should be having in front of our daughter.'

'She doesn't understand,' Imogen snapped, fuming because she knew he was right and she should have thought of the same thing herself. Because, although Nadeena couldn't understand their words, she was soaking up the heightened emotions in the room and that wasn't good.

Sweeping past Nadir, she gasped as she entered a beautifully appointed bedroom with vast ceilings and long ornate keyhole-shaped windows lined with pale floaty curtains. Deep pink fabric was draped over the elaborate king-sized bed but, other than that, the furnishings wouldn't have been out of place in any five-star hotel. A freshly made up cot stood beside the bed.

'I thought you might like to keep Nadeena close.'

She hadn't expected him to show her that level of thoughtfulness.

'Thank you,' she said stiltedly, rubbing her arms against the chill in the air. 'Is it usually so cold?'

'Always.'

Startled by the gravity of his tone, Imogen stared across at him. His hands were shoved into his pockets and the hard planes of his face seemed even more austere, the grimness of his expression making her think he was talking about more than just the air temperature.

'I'll have the thermostat adjusted. Get some sleep. You look tired.'

Excellent. She looked exactly how she felt.

'I have organised clothing and baby-related items for you which should be through the dressing room. If there's anything the staff has missed just let me know.'

'How could you arrange this so quickly?'

'Bakaan might be somewhat of a backwater compared to the Western world, but it does have retail outlets. And Dubai is an hour away by plane. Anything we didn't have they would have.'

'It seems you've thought of everything.'

His eyes were shuttered as he looked at her. 'Let's hope so.'

With a brief glance at Nadeena, who was wide awake and taking in her new surroundings with open curiosity, Nadir left and closed the door softly behind him.

So civilised, she thought, feeling anything but civilised herself.

'Okay, baby girl. What now?'

Deciding to check out the items Nadir had supplied in the dressing room, she was shocked when she saw just how much he had bought.

She lay Nadeena on her tummy on the floor, watching as she slowly pulled herself towards a row of shoe boxes. Curious herself, Imogen lifted the lid on the first box and gasped at the sight of an exquisite pair of designer shoes nestled amongst the tissue paper. They were her size and she wondered how he had known and then she remembered the day he had taken her shopping in Paris. Did he still remember? Probably not. Probably, it had just been a good guess. He did know women, after all.

Not wanting to dwell on that disagreeable topic, she next checked the clothing hanging on the rack. Most of them were Western, with a few traditional-looking dresses amongst them.

There were more clothes on the hangers than in her own wardrobe and she felt uneasy at why he would have supplied so many. Not that she'd wear them. But she would need to change Nadeena and she couldn't suppress her delight at each of the baby outfits his staff had provided. Gorgeous soft cottons and silks, the like of which she hadn't been able to afford herself.

'All this for one day,' she said to Nadeena. 'The man has clearly never had to work to a realistic budget in his life.'

Nadeena answered with a litany of ga-ga noises and upended a box of shoes. Saving the shoes and confiscating the tissue paper, Imogen let her have the empty box, which she immediately started banging on the floor.

Feeling suddenly weary and lost, she changed Nadeena into a soft cotton sleeping suit and fed her. Then she laid her in the cot and grimaced when she saw how wired she was. Sleep looked like a long time coming. Deciding it would be a waste of energy to try to sing her to sleep, she rang Minh instead.

'I was beginning to get worried when I didn't hear from you after your brief text. How are you? How's our darling girl?' he asked.

'Nadeena is fine.' She'd particularly enjoyed Nadir's private jet. 'And I feel like I've been put through a spin dryer ten times. He wants to see her,' she added softly.

She heard Minh settle into his leather sofa and wished she was there with him with a nice bottle of red between them and a rom com on the TV.

'I've already guessed he's the father or you wouldn't be in Bakaan so you know, he does have a right to see her,' he said.

'I know that.' Imogen watched Nadeena stuff the ear of a soft teddy bear into her mouth and chew. 'At least logically I know that.' Emotionally, she wasn't ready to concede the parenting of Nadeena to anyone else but herself and a couple of trusted friends. 'I just never thought he'd be interested in her.'

'Well, he clearly is. And maybe that's a good thing.'

Imogen pulled a face. 'I don't see how.'

'He's a very powerful man. He can provide for her, you know.' Minh's voice grew soft down the end of the phone. 'And no doubt for you as well.'

'I don't want his money.'

'I know that. But you could use someone to take care of you.'

That had been her mother's mistake. It wouldn't be hers. 'And what about love?' She picked

Nadeena up when she saw her yawn and laid her head on her shoulder.

'Are we talking about for Nadeena or for you?'

'Nadeena. The way he looked at me today…' She felt heaviness inside her chest and it was hard to get the words out. 'Believe me, there's no love lost between us.' And she would never want Nadir's love for herself again. She'd got over that unrealistic desire a long time ago.

'Try to look on the bright side,' he said. 'It might not be so bad.'

Imogen released a pent-up breath. Looking on the bright side wasn't exactly her forte. She was more a planning for the worst case scenario kind of girl. It was her safety blanket. It kept her from making mistakes—or being surprised by things. If her own mother had crossed every *t* and dotted every *i* maybe she wouldn't have been so shocked when her father had left them and never came back. Maybe she would have been more prepared.

'He left me when I needed him the most,' she said, wondering why that still had the capacity to hurt. She'd got over that as well, hadn't she? 'How could I ever trust him with Nadeena? With me?'

'That's definitely a black mark against him. But you have to think of what's best for Nadeena now.'

Imogen chewed on her lower lip so hard she tasted blood. '*I'm* what is best for Nadeena. He's nothing more than a playboy prince who comes and goes as he pleases and gets whatever he wants.' Imogen steeled her heart, more resolved than ever to resist him. 'I won't let Nadeena have my childhood and that's all Nadir can offer.'

They talked for a few minutes more, with Minh promising to call her boss and tell him that she wouldn't be in over the next couple of days, and then Imogen focused on getting Nadeena to sleep.

Her conversation with Minh had unsettled her. She'd wanted him to tell her that Nadir was a rat bastard but all he'd done was say things that had flashed across her own mind, which left her more conflicted than ever.

She knew giving in to his demand that she marry him would ultimately end in tears. Most likely Nadeena's. And quite possibly her own. In frustration, if nothing else!

CHAPTER SIX

IN THE END it took her an hour to put Nadeena to sleep and when she went looking for Nadir she wasn't expecting to find him barefoot and shirtless with a dark-haired woman bending over his lap.

The sight shocked her and suddenly a long-lost memory of her fifteen-year-old self flew into her mind. She'd been with a bunch of friends on a school excursion when they had come across her father in a passionate embrace with a woman who wasn't her mother. The woman's hands had been in her father's hair, his hand close to her breast, his mouth devouring hers. Imogen had been stunned. Sickened. The girls with her had giggled nervously and her father hadn't even looked contrite. He'd scowled at her and asked her why she wasn't in school. God, she hadn't remembered that in years.

The woman in the white *abaya* straightened and

Imogen saw she was holding an empty silver tray and a tumbler of Scotch sat on the low table beside the sofa.

Imogen did a double-take when she realised that the woman was a servant who was now retreating from the room. Her mind had put two and two together and come up with ten. Maybe she was more tired than she'd realised...

'You must be Imogen?'

Whirling around at the sound of a deep male voice, Imogen saw a man bearing a striking resemblance to Nadir standing over by the keyhole windows. He looked tall and imposing in his traditional white robes and matching headdress and Imogen knew that there was no way she would have missed him if she hadn't been so riveted by the sight of Nadir's impressive chest.

'Imogen, this is my brother, Zachim. Zach, this is Imogen.'

Zachim nodded, his eyes glinting amber-gold in the softly lit room as he regarded her. 'I remember you from the dance hall and it's a pleasure to finally meet you.'

Feeling trapped by her pent-up emotions and unsure what Nadir had told him, Imogen was uncertain as to how to proceed. It seemed highly improper to let rip with the frustration and angst clawing at the inside of her throat and yet she didn't want to wait till morning to discuss things with Nadir. It seemed important to do so now. 'I'm sorry; I didn't mean to interrupt. Perhaps you can let me know when you're free.'

'I thought you were going to bed?'

The easy familiarity with which Nadir spoke to her in front of his brother made her instantly defensive. 'Why—because you told me to?'

'No. Because you look like you're about to fall over with exhaustion.'

Imogen glared at Nadir and felt even worse when his brother cleared his throat discreetly from behind her. 'I think I should leave you both alone.'

'No, please.' She was horrified at what he must think of her. 'I didn't mean to interrupt you.'

Prince Zachim smiled but it was weary. 'You didn't. My brother is being his usual obstinate self. Maybe you can talk some sense into him. He won't listen to me.'

Imogen was about to say that Nadir didn't listen to her either when he rose from the sofa and the sight of all those hard muscles rippling across his abdomen as he moved made the words fly out of her head.

'I'm not going to change my mind, Zach.'

'It's your birthright.'

'If you're feeling guilty about taking something from me then don't. I don't want anything to do with Bakaan.'

'Nadir, I know you're still angry about the past but—'

Nadir made a motion with his hand that cut his brother off. 'Goodnight, Zach.'

Zachim scowled. 'All right, Nadir, You win this round.'

'Hallelujah.' Nadir's voice held no enthusiasm and Imogen wondered what it was Nadir was still angry about and what exactly Zach was taking from him.

'I have to fly to the mountains early tomorrow,' Zachim said as he turned to go. 'But I'll be back by noon.'

'I'll be waiting.'

Zachim gave her a weary smile. 'Lovely to meet you, Imogen. I'm not sure if I should congratulate you on your impending marriage to my brother or offer commiserations.' His smile held a touch of irony. 'But I definitely look forward to getting to know you and to meeting my niece over lunch tomorrow.'

Imogen smiled warmly. As handsome and dashing as he was, this brother didn't tie her insides up in knots like Nadir did. 'I look forward to it.'

Zach looked back at Nadir as if he wanted to say more but Nadir gave him a faint smile. 'Give it up, Zach. You're perfect for the role and you know it. And stop flirting with my fiancé.'

'Nadir!'

His name left her lips in an appalled reprimand but Zach just laughed heartily.

'You might not like being back in Bakaan, brother, but I like you being here'

Nadir watched his brother give him a mocking salute and stride out of the room and knew that he was doing the right thing in giving Zach the leadership role. They had different mothers and therefore vastly different experiences of their father and their homeland. And it wasn't just anger or resentment at the past that stopped Nadir wanting to be the next King; it was also the painful memories that haunted him every time he was here. It was the sense of guilt his brother would never understand because Nadir had never told him of the cowardly role he'd played in his mother

and sister's deaths. The feelings of shame and in-
eptitude. A feeling of emptiness.

If he'd thought the people of Bakaan really
needed him, if he thought he could add some
value Zach couldn't as leader then he might do
it. But the fact was Zach was a capable military
leader and was perfect for the job.

'I apologise if I ruined your conversation with
your brother. It wasn't my intention.'

He eyed Imogen still standing in the middle
of the room and picked up his Scotch, hoping it
would distract him from his bleak thoughts. He
knew a way she could distract him as well but he
didn't think she'd be as biddable as the Scotch.
Unfortunately. 'You didn't; he was leaving anyway.'

She chewed the inside of her lower lip and he
couldn't take his eyes off the little movement.

'Are you okay?'

Her soft question made him gulp a mouthful
of the fiery liquid and he relished the burn of it
down his throat. No, he wasn't okay. 'Concerned
for my welfare, *habibi*? I'm touched.'

He saw her posture stiffen and regretted taking
his frustration out on her. But hell, she was partly
to blame. Sorting out the leadership issue would

be over and done within a matter of hours. Sorting out the rest of his life with a wife and child... He didn't want to contemplate how long that would take. Particularly given the light of defiance burning hotly in Imogen's eyes. A defiance he had yet to fully understand.

'Don't be,' she responded smartly. 'It was an aberration that won't happen again.'

He smiled. He hadn't realised she was so feisty when they'd been together back in Paris. Back then she'd always been thrilled to see him, delight written all over her expressive face. And it had been catching. For those all too brief weekends he'd been happy too. Perhaps that had been her allure. That and the red-hot chemistry between them. 'Whatever you've got to say can wait until morning.'

'Really?' Her eyebrows arched skyward. 'Because you decreed it, *My Lord*?'

No, she definitely hadn't been this feisty in Paris but part of him—the part that turned caveman every time she was around—liked it a little too much for comfort. 'Yes. That and the dark circles under your eyes which suggest you need sleep more than conversation.'

'I'm sorry you don't approve of the way I look.'

She dipped into a mocking curtsy. 'I'll try to do better next time, *My Lord.*'

'I wouldn't use that term too often,' he advised softly, tossing back another finger of Scotch. 'I might like it.'

She scowled at him but her eyes followed his hand as he rubbed it across his chest and his blood surged as he saw the breath catch in her throat. He'd forgotten Zach had interrupted his shower. Did the sight of him bother her? He'd sure as hell be bothered if she was standing before him half naked. Hell, he was bothered anyway and she still had on her crumpled clothes from earlier.

A spike of conscience needled him. She might still be as beautiful as ever but she really did look worn to the bone. His eyes scanned over her body and came to rest on her chest. And she was braless.

'So, anyway…' She cleared her throat and his eyes rose from her round, full breasts to the pulse point beating like a small trapped bird inside her creamy throat. 'I've looked up some options I'd like to go through with you.'

With his instincts pulling at him to go to her and haul her up against him and tame that defiant look in her eyes until she softened and became once again pliant and wanton in his arms, Nadir forced his mind to recall her words. 'Options' was the only word that had stuck but he knew she wouldn't want to discuss the options he was presently interested in. 'Now is not a good time.'

'I disagree.'

Of course she did. 'You had ample opportunity to talk on the plane. You chose not to.'

She perched on the edge of the sectional sofa and faced him. 'Nadeena was awake the whole time. I didn't want her to realise how tense I was. At this age babies feel everything the mother feels.'

He gave a short laugh. 'If that's true you wouldn't have fooled her. Even a blind man could see you were about ready to snap in half.'

'And whose fault is that?'

'Mine, no doubt. Did she go to sleep easily?'

Her lips tightened. 'Yes, thank you.'

'Thank you?'

'For asking, I suppose.' Frustration flashed in her green eyes. 'I…can we just stay on topic?'

'By all means. But you can stop treating me like a stranger. I'm not.'

'You are.' She rubbed the back of her neck as if it ached and rolled her slender shoulders. 'But I didn't come out here to argue with you.'

Nadir took another swallow of Scotch. 'What did you come out here for?'

The air between them thickened and he nearly said to hell with arguing; it was time to relieve some of the tension between them.

'To talk.'

'I've got a better idea.'

She frowned and he saw the moment the meaning behind his rough words became clear because her gorgeous eyes widened in shock. 'I hope you don't mean what I think you mean.'

'Oh, I definitely mean exactly what you think I mean.'

She gasped softly. 'How can you think about sex at a time like this?'

He thought about sex with her all the time. 'Too soon for you, *habibi*? That's okay. I'm a patient man. I can wait.'

'Look, Nadir—'

'Look, Imogen.' He scrubbed a weary hand across his face. 'I'm not in the mood for a discussion. We can talk tomorrow after one o'clock.'

'Why? What happens at one o'clock?'

At one o'clock one of his pesky loose ends would be resolved. 'It's not important.'

Her eyes narrowed. 'Does it have to do with what your brother was talking about before?'

'It doesn't matter.'

'It seemed to matter to him.'

'He'll get over it.'

Her lashes fluttered down to hide her frustrated gaze. 'Keep your secrets. I don't want to know them anyway.'

'It's not a secret. I have business to sort out in Bakaan that doesn't concern you.'

'Fine.' Her tone implied it was anything but fine. 'Let's stay on topic and discuss something that does concern me.'

'By all means let's stay on topic. Tomorrow.'

Imogen didn't like the way his gaze swept over her and wished she'd kept her bra on after Nadeena had gone to sleep because every time his eyes dropped to her chest her nipples peaked. She just hoped that the lighting from the lamps was low enough that he wouldn't notice. Not that she couldn't see every muscle shifting on his torso. He raised his hand to rub at the smattering of hair on his chest again and Imogen barely resisted the urge to fan herself. *Stay on topic yourself,* she admonished silently.

The last thing she needed right now was to think about the offer he'd just made. Which only reinforced his playboy mentality.

I'm a patient man. I can wait.

So much for her earlier assumption that he didn't want to sleep with her. The man would obviously sleep with anyone but he'd be waiting a long time if he thought he could use her to slake his hunger for a night. Been there, done that and now had the baby to prove it! A baby who didn't need him.

Deciding that starting with that statement would be like waving a red flag at an irritated bull, she went straight to the second half of her plan instead.

'So.' She cleared her throat yet again. 'Given that you said that you wanted to be part of Nadeena's life, I looked up some alternative options for us that don't include marriage.'

'Good for you.'

His response was frosty but at least it cooled the air between them and she wouldn't let it put her off. She narrowed her eyes as he crossed his ankle over his knee and then she calmly folded her hands in her lap. 'So it's obviously not an indepth analysis, but from what I can tell there's legal custody and physical custody and they're quite different from each other.'

'Are they?'

His laconic response reeked of disinterest and Imogen did her best to cap her irritation. 'Yes. They are. Legal custody is about who makes decisions for the child and can be sole or joint and physical custody is about seeing the child. Again, that can be either sole or joint and that breaks down into supervised and unsupervised and even virtual visits nowadays.' She took a deep breath and rushed on before he could interject. 'There's also the issue of how to split the time and it seems that the most popular is for the father to visit the child every second weekend and on public holidays. Unless you want to go the virtual route, of course.'

'Of course.'

Imogen waited for him to say more. When he just smiled and curved his hands behind his head she suspected he was toying with her. 'Well?' she prompted stiffly.

'I can see you've put quite a bit of effort into this.'

Imogen sucked in a litre of air and released it slowly. Perhaps she'd been wrong and he wasn't toying with her. Perhaps he was going to be cooperative and let her go. 'Not really.' She gave him a small smile that seemed to stretch her dry lips to the point of cracking. 'But it's a start.'

And, perversely, the possibility that he might agree with her didn't thrill her the way she had imagined it would. Instead, she felt unaccountably disappointed and realised just how much she still wished that their relationship in Paris could have progressed like so many other happy couples did. Couples like Minh and David, who loved each other so much they would do anything for the other person.

She sighed. What had her mother always said? *If wishes were horses, beggars would ride.* Such an old-fashioned saying, passed down through the generations. Would she pass it on to Nadeena with that same air of inevitability?

'Tell me,' he began conversationally, 'did the Internet mention the custody arrangements for a woman who kept her child's birth a secret from its father?'

No, he was not going to be cooperative and icy shivers tripped down her spine as she saw that she had angered him again 'No,' she bit out tersely.

'Then you're right—' his smile was even tighter

than hers '—when you say that your analysis isn't very complete. And furthermore,' he drawled with icy control, 'while you might be happy sharing custody of our daughter, I am not.'

'I'm not either,' she replied hotly. 'But you're not giving me any other choice.'

'On the contrary; I've given you the best choice there is,' he drawled arrogantly.

'Marrying you?'

She could see instantly that he'd taken offence to her contemptuous tone from the stillness of his big body but dammit, he didn't love her. If he did…if he did then things might be different…

'This is all something you should have thought about before you ran away,' he bit out contemptuously.

'I did not run away,' she retorted. 'I left.'

He made a low noise in the base of his throat that startled her. 'I told you I would return and we'd talk about options.' His eyes glittered dangerously. 'You weren't there.'

'Like abortion?' she spat, remembering how cold she had felt reading his missive. How icy she had felt in his apartment when he had confirmed that yes, he'd have preferred not to be an expectant father.

'No, not that.'

He lost colour and tugged a hand through his hair as if the thought truly horrified him.

'Well, it probably would have happened if you had pushed for that horrible paternity test you told me I had to take.'

His brows drew together. 'A paternity test made sense.'

'Do you have any idea how dangerous those tests are?'

'No, I—'

'About one in three hundred amniocenteses end in miscarriage and I would have needed the earlier test. With the CVS you can double the chance of a miscarriage. But then that would have worked a lot better for you than this, wouldn't it?'

Nadir jumped to his feet, his movements lacking their usual grace. 'For the love of all things holy, Imogen, I would never have put you or our baby's life at risk. You must know that.'

Imogen wrapped her arms around her stomach, all the anger leaching out of her as he stood before her all ferocious and earnest as if he meant what he was saying.

Did he?

She didn't know. What she did know was that

she didn't want to be forced to do something stupid that they would both later regret because Nadeena would be the one to pay the ultimate price when things turned bad. Still, a twinge of regret spiked inside her chest. The way he'd said 'our baby', as if he really felt something for Nadeena already. 'And you would have just accepted that I not take the test, I suppose,' she scoffed.

'Of course I would have accepted it.' He settled his hands on his hips. 'At what stage in our relationship did I ever show you that I was unreasonable?'

Imogen tapped her foot and wanted to say *all the time*. But the truth was that he had never been unreasonable towards her. Ever. He had always been thoughtful and kind. Loving. A lie she couldn't afford to be swayed by again. 'Now. You're being unreasonable now.'

'That's a matter of opinion.'

'Damn it, Nadir.' A flash of renewed irritation surged inside her. 'You can't keep me here against my will.'

'Actually, I can,' he said with all the arrogance of a man born to privilege. 'But I won't.' He paused, ran his hand across his stubbled jaw. 'I will, however, stop you from taking Nadeena away from me again.'

Imogen's insides seized and she knew her face went pale, her breathing laboured. 'I hate you.' Because he'd just effectively narrowed her choices down to marriage to him or give up her child.

He nodded as if this was normal. As if she hadn't dreamt of him and wished in her darkest moments that he wouldn't come for her. Tell her that he missed her. Tell her that he loved her. Tell her that he couldn't live without her. Dreams not worth the sleep they had interrupted.

'A child deserves to be raised by both parents.' He regarded her steadily. 'Or are you going to argue with me about that too?'

'Only if both parents love and want her.'

'I agree.'

Imogen clamped her mouth mutinously closed and turned her attention to the intricate patterns on the Persian rug at her feet before she said something she'd truly regret.

Nadir sighed. 'Believe it or not, Imogen, I only have Nadeena's best interests at heart.'

'Do you?'

'Yes.' She heard a hardness enter his voice at her scepticism.

She looked at him and all the fight left her and a great sense of doom pervaded her limbs. 'And what if a marriage between us is the worst thing for her?'

He looked genuinely perplexed by her question. 'I don't see how it could be.'

'Because it would be nothing but a marriage of convenience.'

'I don't see it that way.'

She blew out a frustrated breath. 'How can you not?'

He stepped in front of her, breathing as hard as she was. 'Because there's nothing remotely convenient about marriage and ours will be real.'

Real? Imogen swallowed heavily and lost her breath. 'I hope you don't mean what I think you mean.'

'We will be man and wife in every sense of the word, *habibi,*' he said softly with the same confidence she had once loved.

Imogen's chin jutted forward. 'I didn't think you were into force.'

She knew that if she revealed just how badly he affected her it would be akin to lying down and waving a white flag. So she held her breath as his eyes ran over her face and down over her throat and willed herself not to move, silently urging her racing heartbeat to slow to a moderate gallop.

As if he couldn't help himself, he raised his hand and brushed his thumb across her lips in a whisper-soft caress that made every one of her nerve endings tingle. For a long moment they just stared at each other and then he ruined the moment by speaking. 'Force, *habibi*?'

The gentle words mocked her and she jerked back and stepped away from him, doing her best to ignore the way the blood pounded heavily through her body and highlighted her inability to control her attraction to him. No man had ever affected her so deeply that she forgot who she was and where she was and she refused to give him that kind of power over her again. It made her feel helpless to follow her own will. It made her hungry to taste him. It made her willing to risk everything. Almost...

Forcing herself to take another slow step backwards, she banked her confused emotions as best she could and reached down deep for reason. 'Be serious, Nadir. A child will completely cramp your lifestyle. They're inconvenient and messy and exhausting and...and...' *Wonderful and joy-*

ous and funny and loving... She swallowed. 'And smelly. Really smelly at times.'

Nadir paced away from her and then turned sharply on his heel. 'I don't understand you. Most women would be jumping for joy at the prospect of having a rich man take care of her and her child.'

'Except I'm not most women and I *know* this is a mistake. My parents married because my mother was pregnant with me and it was a miserable affair for everyone. They stayed together even though my father was seeing another woman because my mother believed a child should be raised by two parents. My father resented being tied to us and after a while I stopped wishing he would pay me attention.'

'I won't resent you.'

Embarrassed at having revealed her deepest wounds to him, Imogen scoffed. 'How can you say that? You have a reputation of being the unobtainable playboy that spans continents.'

His lips thinned into a flat line. 'People see what they want to see. But if you think love is some sort of guarantee of a happy union, it isn't. My parents were the poster children for that particular misconception and they didn't last.'

Imogen frowned. 'I find that hard to believe if it was true love,' she said huskily.

'Believe it. They separated when my father took a second wife and—'

'Took a second wife!'

'Yes, it is the custom that men in Bakaan can take more than one wife.'

'You can definitely forget marriage then.'

He smiled wearily. 'Don't worry. I am not a masochist.'

'Is that supposed to be funny? I think it's appalling that men are allowed to have more than one wife. I bet the women aren't allowed more than one husband.'

'No. And it bothered my mother just as much. In the end they hated each other so much there was never any joy in visiting either one of them. My mother was always trying to get us to prove our love by feeding her information about our father and our father was constantly derogatory about her and wanting to know what she was up to behind his back. It was as if they couldn't let each other go and frankly it was exhausting.'

And no doubt emotionally crippling, Imogen thought. Which was so unlike the picture she had formed in her mind about his childhood. For some reason she had assumed that his life had been full of opulence and fun and the security of belonging to an ancient dynasty. It seemed she had been wrong. At least about the fun and security.

Curiosity made her pause and she wanted to ask him more but he got in first.

'Forget it.' His flinty gaze seemed to penetrate deep into her mind. 'And forget shared custody, Imogen.'

At the reminder of their earlier argument Imogen's spine straightened. 'You're impossible to reason with.'

'That's because you know I'm right.'

Shaking her head, she would have turned away from him then—anything to put some distance between herself and his half-naked body that seemed to beckon her to reach out and touch it—but his hands came down on her shoulders and held her immobile.

Imogen trembled and knew he felt it by the satisfied gleam that seemed to soften his gaze. 'I've never stopped wanting you, Imogen, and that kiss back in my apartment proves we share an incredibly strong chemistry. Why fight it?'

Realising with a pang that she was held captive under his unwanted spell, Imogen wrenched herself out of his hold and swung away from him. Embarrassed at how easily she became enthralled by him, how easily she succumbed to his words, his touch, she let anger at him, at herself, at the whole world take hold. 'You want to know why?' She squared off in front of him. 'Because, no matter what happens, I have no intention of marrying you and because, despite what you believe, a marriage based on sex will always be weak.'

'Perhaps. But you're a smart girl and you must realise that a marriage based on mutual chemistry and shared interests has strength.'

Imogen didn't feel very smart right now. She felt wrung out and beaten. 'And what do you think that we *share*, Nadir?' she all but spat at him, desperate to lash out at him in any way that she could. Desperate to alleviate the giant ball of emotion welling up inside her and threatening to burst right out of her. 'That could possibly hold a marriage between us together?'

She slapped her hands on her hips and waited for his response but she should have known that he'd have an answer poised on his lips that would floor her. She should have known that a man whose negotiation skills in the business world were second to none would have something up his sleeve to make her feel as big as a thimble.

'Nadeena.' He paused to let his words sink in. 'We have Nadeena.'

CHAPTER SEVEN

AFTER WAITING FOR Zach inside the council chambers for nearly an hour it was safe to say that Nadir was now extremely irritated. Yes, he'd managed to field a few important work calls while he waited but there was only so much he could get done from a country with limited Internet resources.

He also needed to sort things out with Imogen but she'd steadfastly avoided him all morning and frankly he hadn't tried that hard to challenge her on it. Last night's discussion—hell, argument—had played heavily on his mind and made sleep impossible.

Before picking her up yesterday he'd expected to find that she'd aborted his baby, mainly, it had to be said, because she hadn't approached him for a truckload of money and for a while yesterday he'd continued to think that maybe she was somehow playing him for a fool. He'd continued to believe that she had run from him because she'd had something to hide.

He didn't think that now. She was too earnest in her attempts to get him to change his mind about their marriage. Too earnest in her belief that he had been the one to do the wrong thing by her and not the other way around.

He recalled her fierce expression when she'd mentioned his text. At the time he hadn't contemplated the possibility that she would be upset by it. He hadn't contemplated the possibility that she would feel abandoned by his return to New York and feel as if she had to deal with her pregnancy alone. Guilt knifed through him.

He supposed, if he was honest, he'd been mostly to blame because he hadn't communicated his feelings to her, but how the hell was he supposed to have done that when he didn't know how he had been feeling?

Dealing with emotions had never been his strong suit, even before his mother and sister had died.

He remembered his mother encouraging him to embrace that side of his nature and his father telling him it was dangerous and it had been his father who had been proved right.

Nadir sighed. He'd never seen the benefit of re-hashing the past and he still didn't. A man either took action or he bowed out of the game. Nadir had no intention of bowing out. Not with Imogen at any rate.

He glanced at the admiral's chair his father used to occupy at the end of the room during council meetings. As heir to the throne he had always been encouraged to sit in on those meetings and he'd loved them. He'd loved listening to his father taking charge and issuing orders. Watching him handle political issues.

His father had openly shared this side of himself and it wasn't until Nadir had left Bakaan that he'd realised how isolated and increasingly paranoid his father had become. How only a select few were ever allowed into his inner sanctum and then only if those select few agreed with him. From the age of twelve Nadir had started to do that less and less and that was when the rot had set in. That was when his father had started trying to keep him from his mother and sister, explaining that the ties he found the hardest to cut were the ones that needed to be cut most of all.

He rubbed a hand across his face. One of the issues between him and Imogen was that she was, at heart, an emotional and sensual woman who didn't hold back. It was both a draw and a deterrent—although right now he was honest enough to admit that the draw side was definitely winning out. Probably it had been too long since he'd had a woman. It wasn't natural for a healthy male to go without sex for fourteen months.

Hell.

Did he owe Imogen an apology for his behaviour back then? It wasn't a position he had found himself in for years and the last two people he'd needed to apologise to were dead.

Out of the corner of his eye he noticed one of his father's senior council members break away from the group and, like a drowning man grasping for a life raft, he welcomed the interruption to his thoughts.

Old and set in his ways, Omar had never been on Nadir's list of favourite people but he was knowledgeable and, as far as he was aware, loyal to a fault.

'Well?'

'We don't know where he is, Your Highness. He's not answering his phone.'

Nadir gritted his teeth. His brother had said he needed to go into the mountains on some business or other. He'd flown the helicopter himself. Now he was nowhere to be seen and the helicopter was still at the airfield. There was no sign of foul play or anything amiss. 'Fine—we'll proceed without him.'

'I'm afraid that's not possible, Your Highness.'

'Why not?'

'In order for you to renounce your position as King, we need to have your successor present.'

'Well, he's not here and I have a business to run.'

'The council understand, Your Highness,' he said in a way that let Nadir know they didn't understand at all. 'But you are still our acting King and there is a UAE dinner tonight that has been planned for months. It is too late to cancel. Many of the heads of state have already flown into Bakaan. It was quite a coup for Prince Zachim to arrange it. Many will be staying all week on official business.'

'Then Zachim should be here to run it,' Nadir bit out.

'Indeed, Your Highness.' Omar nodded deferentially.

Aware that he was being manipulated but knowing that he was boxed in until Zachim returned, Nadir muttered a curse. 'Okay, I'll do it.

'Very good, Your Highness. And shall I set a place for your wife?'

Nadir's gaze sharpened on the older man. 'Why would you do that?'

'Because spouses have been invited to the dinner. As everyone has heard about your wife, they will expect to see her there.'

Nadir had a good idea how Imogen was going to take that news. 'Try calling my brother again.'

'Of course, Your Highness.'

Nadir paced again while Omar dialled his phone. Most likely it wouldn't work, given the rudimentary telecom system his father had installed in the country. That was another possible reason why no one could reach Zachim. Either that or his brother was hiding out in some attempt to get him to step into the role as leader.

Nadir stilled. Was that it? Was Zach forcing his hand? He frowned as the idea sprouted roots and leaves. As a child, Zachim had often run away and hidden when he was in trouble, waiting for their father's wrath to subside before coming out again. By then Nadir had usually copped Zach's share of the punishment as well as his own so it wasn't a bad strategy—one Nadir had been too proud to ever try himself—but it was quite possible that Zach was right now holed up somewhere with a woman and a case of wine. If he was… Nadir shook his head. If he was, he'd beat him to a pulp when he returned.

'No luck, Your Highness.'

'Fine. Set a place for Imogen.' Nadir turned to leave the room, already thinking about what needed to be done before the evening dinner when Omar's next words stopped him cold.

'And your wedding?'

'Excuse me?'

'Your wedding? You may have forgotten but a Western marriage is not recognised as legal for a member of the royal family. It would be best, Your Highness, if you formalised the marriage in a traditional ceremony as soon as possible.'

Hoping that the issue of his legal ties to Imogen wouldn't have arisen in the small amount of time he was supposed to be in Bakaan, Nadir sighed. 'I suppose you have a perfect date available, Omar?'

'As soon as possible, Your Highness. There is some unrest in the northern part of the country and some who would wish to destabilise the throne. It is important that the people observe their crown prince behaving in a way befitting the leadership.'

'You know I do not intend to become the next leader of Bakaan, Omar, so the timing doesn't matter,' Nadir said tightly.

'As you wish, Your Highness.'

Realising that he was being obstinate and the council members had no idea why he didn't want the damned leadership role, Nadir softened his position. 'I know you're worried, Omar, but don't be. Zachim will most likely be back before the evening meal is served. In the meantime, if you think that formalising my marriage is absolutely necessary then organise the ceremony for a week from today.'

That would give Zach plenty of time to stop playing his games—if he was actually staying away on purpose—and get back here. And on the off-chance he was still holding out on him in a week then they would marry. It wasn't any big deal because it was going to happen, one way or another.

'I'm sorry—who did you say you were?'

Imogen placed Nadeena in the baby recliner beside the beautifully paved swimming pool and fastened the safety catch, the fronds of the palm trees overhead keeping the scorching sun from burning her. When she was done she turned to the two women standing in the open doorway. One was young and striking-looking in the traditional cream-coloured outfit that denoted the palace servants and the other woman was much older and dressed in faded black garments. And her eyes were transfixed by Nadeena.

'My name is Tasnim and this is Maab,' the younger one said with a wide smile 'We are your servants, My Lady.'

'Oh.' Imogen smiled kindly. Used to fending for herself and preferring it that way, she had no need for servants. 'Thank you, but—'

Before she could say anything, Maab had moved closer to Nadeena and was crooning something in Arabic. As if sensing Imogen's regard, she turned and bowed her head, speaking in rapid Bakaani.

'I'm sorry,' Imogen said, 'I don't understand.'

'Please excuse Maab, My Lady. She does not speak very much English but she is excellent with babies and helped raise the royal siblings when they were little. She is asking if she might approach the little princess.'

'Well, of course she can.' Imogen smiled encouragingly and the old woman knelt down in front of Nadeena and gasped in surprise. She started spouting the name Sheena and smiling broadly.

Confused, Imogen turned to Tasnim for clarification.

'Maab says that the little princess looks just like Sheena.'

'Sheena?'

'The King's sister, My Lady.'

'Oh, Nadir's aunt? That's nice.'

Tasnim gave her a funny look. 'No, My Lady, she means King Nadir's sister.'

Imogen was silent for a moment as she processed that piece of information. She'd never heard of Nadir having a sister but that wasn't surprising, really. Their short relationship in Paris hadn't progressed past the intensely sexual phase and, whether by accident or design, neither of them had wasted their time talking about family or personal history. For Imogen that had been deliberate. She hadn't wanted to talk about her mother's recent death and her father's remarriage a month later. Had Nadir chosen not to speak about his past because he was upset by it as well?

'The King has asked me to help you prepare for the evening ahead. Would you like to do that now, My Lady?'

The evening ahead? Feeling as if her life was once again spinning out of her control and not wanting to look like a complete dill, Imogen kept her expression bland. 'By King you mean... Nadir?'

'*Na'am*, My Lady. Yes.'

A sudden sense of unease fluttered up from her stomach. Nadir couldn't be King because if he was that would mean they were going to be here for a *little* longer than a day, but if he wasn't then why were these women even here?

'I think there must be some mistake,' she began slowly and then Zach's words jumped into her head from the night before.

It's your birthright.

Was Nadir here to discuss some sort of succession planning? She hadn't contemplated that and perhaps he would expect her to meet his father. She nearly grimaced. It was one thing to meet his brother but if his father was anything like her own then he was unlikely to approve of her.

Maab started saying something again in Arabic and there was a hint of pride in her voice.

'Maab says that we are delighted that he has come back, My Lady. That King Nadir will be a great king because he was a great boy. Kind and loyal and very strong.'

Imogen had no doubt that Nadir had been strong but she wasn't so sure about the kind and loyal part. *Ruthless and self-serving?* Now that she would have believed in an instant and she wasn't sure how she felt hearing this woman's hero worship of a man she was convinced was set on doing the right thing because of a *guilty* conscience rather than a *good* one.

'That's lovely,' she murmured.

Tasnim nodded. 'She was very sad to think that Nadir would not return after the death of his father.'

'The death of his father?'

Tasnim gave her another funny look and Imogen's pride kicked in. 'Oh, yes, the death of his father.'

What the heck was going on here?

'It has been a troubling two weeks for those of us working in the palace,' Tasnim continued. 'And not knowing what would happen…but I'm sorry, My Lady, you don't want to hear all this.'

Not want to hear it? Imogen wanted to hear that and more. She could hardly believe what Tasnim had said so far. Had Nadir's father truly died two weeks ago? And what did that mean? Was Nadir going to be King? Did he expect Imogen to move to Bakaan? The whole concept was totally implausible and she could feel panic threatening. She needed to speak to Nadir to sort this out. Right now.

Giving Tasnim what she hoped was a benign smile, she said, 'Thank you, Tasnim. Would you mind telling *my husband* that I don't need any help and I'd really like to see him?'

'Your wish is my command, *habibi*.'

Swinging around at the sound of Nadir's voice, Imogen's jaw nearly hit the floor at the sight of him dressed in flowing black robes that made him look like a pirate. Absurd excitement gripped her and rational thought was whisked away on the light, hot breeze.

And she wasn't the only female affected by the sight of him because Maab rushed to her feet with the agility of a woman half her age and threw herself on the ground in front of him.

'Maab.' Nadir raised the woman and hugged her tightly, speaking to her in his native language, his tone warm and deep. Tears sparkled in the old woman's eyes and, seeing it, Imogen felt tears as well; her emotions much closer to the surface since her daughter had been born.

She wasn't sure what Nadir had said to the women but moments later they had bowed low to them both and disappeared as quickly as they had arrived.

Nadir's gaze swept over her and a small frown of disapproval immediately knitted his brow. 'Why aren't you wearing the clothing I provided?'

Tense and uncertain after what she'd just heard, Imogen was in no mood to talk about fashion. 'Forget the clothing. Why did you lie to me?'

'I did not lie to you. I have never lied to you.'

'You told me we would be leaving today and I've just heard that I'm supposed to be attending a dinner. And that you're the King.' She peered at him, looking for signs that something had changed. 'You're not really the King, are you?'

'No, I'm not the King,' he said in a way that didn't convince her at all.

'Then why do those two women call you the King?'

'Because they believe that I soon will be, I suppose.'

'But why would they think that?'

His face turned grim and Imogen felt worry spike inside her. 'A glitch.'

'A glitch?'

'Nobody is King until the coronation but in the meantime the country needs someone to lead it. I am acting head of state until Zachim returns.'

'So, it's true that your father died recently.'

He shoved his hands into the pockets of his robe. 'It's true.'

Imogen didn't know what to say in the face of his implacable regard. 'I'm sorry for your loss.'

'Don't be.' He drew a weary hand across his jaw. 'The whole purpose of my return to Bakaan was not to take over the throne but to cede it to Zachim.'

'Oh.' Didn't he want to be King? And if not, why not? 'I suppose, given that women aren't allowed multiple husbands in Bakaan, your sister isn't allowed to take over the throne instead.'

'My sister?' A muscle flickered in his jaw. Once. Twice. 'Who told you about my sister?'

Not wanting to get the young servant into trouble, Imogen hesitated. 'Tasnim. But don't blame her. I pushed for the information.'

'Then you didn't push hard enough.' His expression made her feel chilled. 'My sister is no longer alive either.'

'Oh, God, I'm so sorry.' Imogen felt stricken as she saw a mask of pain briefly cross his face. 'Did she die with your father?'

'No.' Nadir expelled a harsh breath, his emotions hidden behind the screen of his impossibly long eyelashes. 'But you are right. She would not have been allowed to be a sheikha.' His lashes raised and she could see that his emotions were now firmly under control. 'Now, since Zachim has disappeared for the moment, I must attend a state dinner tonight and I need you to accompany me.'

'But what about our return to London?'

'It has been delayed.'

'It can't be delayed. I have a job I need to get back to and we're really short-staffed at the café.'

Nadir gave her a dry look. 'You will no longer need that job, Imogen, so you might as well quit.'

Imogen shoved her hands onto her hips. 'I will not quit.'

Nadir let out a long sigh. 'I hope to Allah that not every conversation we have is going to feel like I'm pulling out hen's teeth. If you go into your dressing room you will find an evening gown for the dinner and Tasnim will help you prepare. If you need anything else—'

'Nadir, every conversation feels like a struggle because you won't listen. And I'm not going anywhere with you tonight when nothing has been resolved between us.'

'Of course it has. We resolved everything last night.'

As far as Imogen was concerned, they had resolved nothing last night. 'When?'

'When we talked.'

She shook her head, frustrated that he could be so obtuse. 'You might have resolved something last night but I didn't.'

His sigh was one of aggravated patience. 'Okay, tell me what you need to make this work for you.'

Was he serious? 'Time.' *For one thing.* 'You listening to what I want would help.'

Nadir pulled a wry face. 'I promise to try and listen to you but unfortunately I can't do anything about your first request because time is something I seem to be in short supply of right now. And I have never seen the point in stalling when the outcome is not in question.'

His high-handedness was one of the things that had attracted her to him so she really only had herself to blame. 'I take it you mean the outcome of us marrying and if you do then the outcome is only not in question for you.'

'For us.'

'This is what I would call not listening,' she said with exasperation. 'Because at this point there is no us. There is you and me and a baby. I mean—what about where we're going to live? What about what school Nadeena will go to? What about her emotional well-being?'

His crooked grin made her breath catch and she wondered if that wasn't exactly the outcome he'd been trying to achieve. 'You will live where I live. Nadeena will go to a good school and we both want what is best for her.'

'You're simplifying.'

'And you're making it complicated.' It was he who sounded exasperated now.

'It *is* complicated.'

'It doesn't have to be.'

Imogen's eyes shot to his as the tenor in his voice roughened and, just like that, sex was in the room again. Or at least in her thoughts. 'Be serious, Nadir—we don't even like each other any more.'

'I like you.'

About to tell him that what he thought of her
was inconsequential anyway, she found the words
dissolving on her tongue as she watched him hun-
ker down and start trickling water over Nadeena's feet. Nadeena reached forward and grabbed
one of his thick fingers in her chubby hand. Imogen closed her eyes and then opened them again
when Nadeena giggled and splashed the water
with her feet.

Nadir smiled. That smile that had melted a thousand hearts, including her own.

They looked so beautiful together. Her daughter
and the man who had once made her so impossibly happy she'd thought she would burst. Both
dark-haired and with goofy smiles. Nadir started
saying something softly to Nadeena in Arabic and
Imogen felt that strange tug in her chest she knew
was a type of longing. A type of longing that she
really didn't want to feel again.

'Don't you want more?' The words were out of
her mouth before she knew she was even about
to say them and when Nadir looked up her heart
stuttered at how incredibly virile he looked.

His eyes skimmed over her and if she wasn't
mistaken lingered on her lips. Heat suffused her
cheeks. 'More what?'

Imogen didn't want to say it but it was as if someone else was directing her mouth. 'Love. Don't you want to marry for love?'

His grimace spoke volumes. 'Love is for greeting cards and grandmothers, not for marriage.'

'Which shows you how wrong we are for each other because I only want to marry for love.'

'I already told you my parents married for love. It caused nothing but grief.'

She could tell by his tone that he was deadly serious. 'You really believe that, don't you?'

'No, I know it. Otherwise you would not still be arguing with me and resisting this marriage. You would be embracing the fact that I can give you a life few others can.' His mouth tilted mockingly at the corners. 'Including your *friend* back in London.'

Ignoring his last comment, Imogen was shocked by his view. 'You would prefer that I marry you for your money? That's so cold and…empty.'

'It's honest.' He gave a frustrated shake of his head, keeping his face soft for Nadeena's sake. 'And tonight is important, Imogen. Or I wouldn't ask.'

She swallowed and lifted her eyes to his.

'Why?' she asked bleakly. 'I got the impression that Bakaan doesn't mean anything to you.'

'That's complicated too.'

'How?'

His face closed down and she knew he wouldn't answer her.

'Let's just say that it is and leave it at that.'

'So much for listening,' she muttered.

He looked at her. 'I have answered every question you've asked.'

'You think?'

He rubbed a hand across his jaw. He needed a shave, she thought absently, and how was it possible for his mouth to be such a perfect bow? He caught her staring and awareness pulsed between them.

The kiss they had shared the day before jumped into her mind and by the way his eyes had now dropped to her own mouth she suspected it had jumped into his as well.

His silent scrutiny unnerved her and she moved sideways to get around him and hoped to heaven that he didn't touch her because she wasn't sure how she'd react if he did. Or at least she *was* sure but she didn't want to have that reaction. She had a horrible way of mixing sex up with love when it came to this man and given his miserable views on love it would be emotional suicide for her to risk her heart—and Nadeena's—on him again.

'My country suffered a great deal because of my father's reign. I will not worsen that by ignoring my current duties. Now, as much as I *enjoy* arguing with you, we are out of time. Will you come with me tonight?'

It wasn't really a question. 'Do you always have to be so pushy?' she complained.

A cloud came across his face and, just like that, he was a stranger again. 'I will watch Nadeena while you get ready.'

Frustrated at the way he just seemed to corral her into a corner as if she was a rogue horse, she tried to think of some way out. 'She needs a bath.'

'Then I will give her one.'

'By yourself?'

'Don't look so surprised. I doubt it's rocket science but if it makes you feel better I will have Maab present so that Nadeena can bond with her.'

Outdone by his logic, Imogen gnashed her teeth. 'It will be a mistake taking me.'

'Why do you say that?'

Because she had no experience of dealing with world leaders and dignitaries and she'd likely embarrass them both. 'I'm a dancer. I danced at the Moulin Rouge. Surely everyone will think I'm unsuitable to be the wife of a king.'

'No doubt some will.'

That stung and his ready agreement was like the flick of a knife across a wound that hadn't quite healed.

He glanced at her impatiently. 'But I won't be King so it doesn't matter.'

'Why not? Too much responsibility for you?'

He shoved his hand through his hair and turned it into a sexy mess. 'Are you trying to annoy me to get me to change my mind about our union?'

'Would it work?'

'No.' His brow quirked with a mixture of frustration and humour. 'Now, stop with the delaying tactics. Nadeena will be fine and, as beautiful as you undoubtedly are, yesterday's jeans and T-shirt aren't going to work tonight.'

'I hate you,' she said, but the words lacked the heat they had carried the day before and by the way he smiled he knew it.

'I got that memo last night. Now, let's get this duty over and done with, hmm?'

Yes, Nadir was all about duty but Imogen knew that duty was a poor motivator that led to anger and neglect and resentment unless it was backed up by something deeper and she feared that was exactly where they were headed if she conceded to his demands.

CHAPTER EIGHT

'KID, THAT'S SOME pitching arm you've got on you.' Nadir leant down and picked up the ball Nadeena had lobbed from her high chair for the millionth time. It was a game she never seemed to tire of. 'I can see you being a softball star when you're older.'

She babbled gleefully when he placed the soft fabric ball back in front of her but, instead of throwing it straight away, she reached towards him with a big grin and tried to grab his *keffiyeh.* 'Not that.' He grinned down at her and pushed his headdress back over his shoulder. 'I've explained that it doesn't look so good scrunched up by grubby baby hands.' Redirecting her attention to the ball, he checked his Rolex again and spied the empty doorway.

If Imogen didn't show up soon they wouldn't have time to stop for him to give her the ring that was burning a hole in his pocket and he didn't want her facing a room full of dignitaries and gossips without it. And somehow it seemed important to solidify things between them. Important to remind her that she was with him now and always would be.

Their earlier conversation and her look of surprise when she'd asked him if he wanted more— and he'd said no—replayed in his head. For a moment she'd looked so vulnerable that he'd wanted to snatch the words back but there had been enough misunderstanding between them and he didn't want there to be any more. But he supposed he should have realised that she was a romantic. That she would want love. It still irked him that she had said she didn't want to marry without it because clearly she didn't love him and he didn't love her.

Which did not mean that their marriage was doomed. He had feelings for her and she might not think great sex was any reason to get married but it was a start and he knew she wasn't as immune to him as she tried to pretend to be. Hell, that kiss had been proof enough of that, as was the way she held herself so carefully whenever he got close to her.

Nadeena clapped her chubby hands together

with delight when he returned the ball to her yet again. 'If only your mother was so easily pleased,' he said softly.

She blew him a raspberry and he stroked his hand over her silky head. His daughter was a revelation to him—as was the depth of his feelings for her. Which only made him more determined to forge ahead with this marriage. Nadeena would not suffer the division of two parents' expectations for her the way he and his sister had.

As she babbled at the ball again as if she might direct it from sheer will alone, Nadir grinned and felt his heart clench at her trusting gaze. He dropped a kiss on top of her head, turning when he heard the swish of fabric behind him.

Only to have his heart clench all over again.

Imogen stood framed in the doorway wearing a blue silk floor-length gown that on the hanger had looked beautiful. On her it looked extraordinary. Her slender dancer's arms and the graceful line of her neck was exposed to his gaze, her hair a soft fall of golden waves around her shoulders. She looked every bit a royal princess. Every bit a woman any man would want on his arm. In his bed.

'I think this is going to be too much for Nadeena. She didn't sleep well last night.'

Nadir couldn't take his eyes off her. 'Do you mean you didn't?'

Imogen's mouth tightened. Her face looked pale and he could see the pulse in her throat going crazy. It bobbed as she swallowed and he couldn't control the wave of tenderness that overcame him in that moment. Imogen—fearless Imogen who took him on at every turn—seemed truly daunted by the prospect of the evening ahead. Or was it something else? Him, perhaps?

It annoyed him that she was so set on ignoring the chemistry between them that pulled tight every time they were together. As far as he was concerned, that was the *only* thing really working for them right now and he'd happily embrace it if she would.

'I've never left Nadeena with a stranger before.' She gripped her hands together tightly. 'She's always had the neighbour across the street or Minh.'

The mention of her ex-lover seemed to wipe any rational thought from his brain. In fact imagining her with any other man did that... 'She will be fine.'

'My daughter *needs* me.'

'*Our* daughter,' he said impatiently. 'And she's just had two hours to get used to Maab and she seems genuinely happy with her.'

'Two hours! It takes more than that to feel comfortable with someone.'

It hadn't taken him five minutes to feel comfortable with her. 'The grand ballroom is in the west wing, only a few minutes from here.'

'I think I feel sick.'

Sympathy replaced irritation. This was all new for her; he had to remember that. 'I will be by your side, *habibi*.'

She threw him a pithy glance. 'Is that supposed to be of comfort?'

Yes, it had been. 'Should I have told you that you will be on your own and if you make a mistake you'll receive a thousand lashes?'

'I might have believed that.'

Her dry sense of humour had drawn him from the start and right now he wanted to laugh, shake her and kiss her all at the same time. 'Come.'

She stood stock-still. 'I am not a dog, Nadir.'

'No, you are a stunning woman who is trying her best to rile me,' he said softly. 'Fortunately for you, I have infinite control.' Usually, he amended. Usually, when she wasn't in the room, shredding it. He watched her wide, kohl-lined green eyes sparkle and then drop behind a veil of ebony lashes. Did she have any idea how incredibly beautiful she was to him? How much he wanted to possess her? How much he wanted to haul her into his arms and eat that pink gloss right off her lips? Having his old nanny and his daughter in the same room helped prevent it. But only just. 'We need to go.'

If possible, she angled her chin higher. 'To London?'

'Not quite. But I admire your humour.' He opened the door and beckoned for her to precede him.

She walked over to kiss their daughter before speaking to Maab. 'If she cries at all then you'll come and get me?'

'*Na'am*, My Lady.'

'Immediately?'

'*Na'am*, My Lady.'

Her gaze looked troubled when she neared him. 'I notice they say that a lot,' she whispered. 'Can I trust her?'

God, she was breathtaking. 'Nothing will happen to Nadeena. Relax.'

* * *

Relax? Impossible. She was too acutely aware of the way Nadir's regal robes brushed against the skirt of the amazing dress he had provided for her and the sense of power he effortlessly exuded. Walking beside him, it was hard to remember that none of this was real and that she didn't want it to be real.

Or did she?

The moment Nadir had leant forward and kissed the top of Nadeena's head as he played with her jumped into her consciousness and her heart lurched inside her chest. It had been identical to the thousands of kisses she had deposited on her daughter's head herself—an instinctive and unconscious gesture of love. Was it possible she was wrong about Nadir? Was it possible he might one day love their daughter as deeply as she did?

Feeling confused and out of her depth, her steps faltered as they entered a grand atrium with exquisite inlaid arabesque carvings on the ceilings and walls and highly polished bronze flooring. Six elaborately dressed Bakaani guards stood to attention with guns strapped to their hips. One of the men glanced briefly at Nadir and stepped forward, his hand poised on a gilt-edged doorknob.

Imogen swallowed heavily, aware that she had no experience of this kind of thing, and insecurity and a deep sense of inadequacy fought it out for top position in her mind.

Stopping beside her, Nadir delved into a hidden pocket in his robe, muttering something about 'earlier' under his breath. Then he turned towards her and held out a ring with a stone the size of a small grapefruit—an oval-shaped diamond grapefruit that was exquisitely hand-crafted and the most divine piece of jewellery Imogen had ever seen. Both her heart and her mind did a double-take.

'Before we go in you'll need to put this on.'

Momentarily blank, she stared at it.

'It's an engagement ring.'

She knew what it was. Sometimes as a young girl she had imagined receiving one from a man she loved. She and her friends had even gone engagement ring shopping once when they had been bored after school. They had then dreamed up elaborate ways their future beaus might pop what had felt like the biggest question of their lives back then. At no time had any of them come up with the man of their dreams saying, 'You'll need to put this on.'

And how many times was she going to get her hopes up over this man only to have them dashed by the reality that he was here because she was the mother of his baby and for no other reason?

'That's not necessary,' she said huskily, instinctively snatching her hands behind her back.

A frown drew down his brows as if her reluctance hadn't occurred to him. 'Of course it is. Many of the guests at the dinner are Western. They will expect to see you wearing my ring.'

A sickening sense of inevitability crept over Imogen and made her feel incredibly vulnerable. Incredibly exposed. 'I can say I lost it if anyone asks.'

His frown turned into a scowl. 'If it's the fact that you didn't choose it yourself that's the problem you can swap it at a later date.'

That wasn't the problem. The problem was that she didn't want to swap it. The problem was that the ring was exactly what she would have chosen had he given her the choice. But he never would. The ruthless way he kept sweeping aside her insistence that she would not marry him as if it was nothing more than an empty spider's web dangling in a doorway was evidence of that alone.

'You have no idea, do you?' she tossed at him,

wanting to somehow hurt him the way he was currently hurting her. 'I don't want to wear your ring because it will ruin it when someone who really loves me wants to give me one.'

Swearing under his breath, Nadir's expression grew stormy. 'Damn it, Imogen, there won't be anyone else putting a ring on your finger. So you can get that out of your mind right now.'

She shook her head, aware that they were studiously *not* being watched by the guards who stood to attention around them. As if sensing her discomfort, or uncomfortable himself, Nadir drew her to the side of the room in what probably looked like a loving gesture.

'I thought I had explained how important tonight was.'

'You don't explain things, Nadir, you talk until you get what you want.'

'I *have* explained.' His tone was marked with frustration. 'I was supposed to renounce the throne today but Zach didn't show up. Now I have to host a dinner.'

'But why don't you want to be King? Zach said it was your birthright.'

He shut down. She saw it instantly in the set of his jaw. 'The why is not important. It's the intention that counts. I don't want the job. Zach does. I suppose you intend to be difficult about this as well.'

Hurt by the implication that she was being difficult just for the sake of it, she flinched. 'I'd like to understand it.'

'Do you want to be Queen—is that it?'

'No, that's not it. I didn't even think about that until just then.'

He looked at her.

'I didn't. Why would I when I haven't even agreed to marry you?'

She'd be flattered at his insistence on marrying her if she thought there was any deep sentiment behind it. Basically, it was because of Nadeena with great sex thrown in as a side order.

Without warning, Nadir reached out and raised her chin so that her eyes met his. Instead of looking fierce and commanding he looked frustrated and weary and her heart lurched.

'I need you to cut me some slack here, Imogen. I feel like I'm holding on by a thread.'

The raw words and his pained expression gave her pause but she was loath to let her heart soften towards him because he'd likely trample on it without even noticing.

Of course the traitorous organ didn't listen to her head. It never did when he was around. When he was this close to her that his scent wound its way inside her and made her ache to lean in and press her face into his neck.

'What is it, Imogen?' His thumb drew light circles across her chin, the gesture more comforting than sexual. 'What are you thinking?'

The width of his broad shoulders blocking the soldiers from her view established a feeling of intense intimacy between them and it was as if the dinner guests on the other side of the large doorway didn't exist. 'Honestly, Nadir, I don't know what to think.' She looked up at him and knew that her expression was troubled. 'I don't know what to feel or what to do any more. This is all so confusing and unexpected. One minute I'm alone with Nadeena and then... And what we had in Paris.' She swallowed heavily and his frown deepened. 'It was so...so...' She couldn't say it. She couldn't say that it was so special. That she had counted the minutes from Monday to Friday during that month they had been together and prayed that he would fly in and rap on her front door and kiss her even before he said hello. 'And now I'm scared because everything feels so broken.'

Broken like her own home life had been. Like her heart had been after he had left Paris and like she feared it would be again if she let her guard down and agreed to marry him.

Nadir cupped her face, gently smoothing his fingers along her jaw line, stroking the velvety skin beneath her earlobes.

'Imogen, look at me.' The whispered words were fierce and oh, so close to her ear she could feel his warm breath stirring her hair. She could feel the tips of her breasts pressed lightly against the front of his robes. She stopped breathing as his voice washed over her in deep, melodic waves, her eyes riveted to his as her emotions surged to the surface. 'Do not be scared. I promise you that I will take care of everything. You…Nadeena. I will protect you and provide for you.' He tilted her chin up with the tip of his finger when her eyes fell away from his. 'You will want for nothing, *habibi*. Not clothing or food or shelter.' He searched her face. 'Not diamonds or holidays or palaces. Whatever your heart desires I will give to you. What more is there?'

Love, Imogen thought achingly. Trust. Companionship. *Friendship.* And while she could see that he meant what he said, she knew that he was unlikely to feel those things for her and she was so afraid that she already did for him.

Imogen looked up and found that his silvery-blue eyes had turned stormy with emotion, dark with desire. His nostrils flared. She felt the change in the taut lines of his body and an answering response immediately swept through her own and made her feel soft and weak.

Force majeure, the French dancers had called him and they weren't wrong. He was an irresistible power, a force of nature, and Imogen was like a house of straw caught up in the devastating storm of his masculinity. The devastating storm of his self-assurance.

The hand at her hip moved to the small of her back, pressing her so close it was bordering on indecent. Her gaze shifted to his mouth. His lips parted and hers did the same. Would he kiss her? Here? Now?

'What do you say, Imogen? Will you give us a chance? For Nadeena.'

Imogen felt as if a lead weight had landed inside her chest. He wanted this for their daughter, who bound them together and divided them at the same time. She knew that if she continued to say no it would be beyond selfish because Minh had been right. Nadir did have a right to their daughter and she could either dwell on the past or try to embrace the future.

Feeling as if she was standing on the edge of a precipice with no clear landing over the side, she held out her left hand. 'Okay, Nadir.' She swallowed heavily. 'For Nadeena.'

With only the briefest of hesitations, Nadir took her hand in his and slid the ring into place. Imogen stared at it, cold and heavy on her finger, and willed her heart to stay uninvolved this time.

CHAPTER NINE

NADIR DISMISSED MAAB after she gave him a full report on Nadeena's well-being at the end of the evening and circled the living room waiting for Imogen to return from checking on her.

In many ways they were just like any other couple returning home at the end of an evening out. One saw to the sitter, the other checked on the baby.

He glanced towards the drinks cabinet and thought about pouring them a glass of brandy. If they really were just like any other couple they would take advantage of the fact that the baby was sleeping and maybe have a nightcap before falling all over each other as soon as possible.

Nadir's eyes tracked down over Imogen as she stepped into the room, the evening gown flowing around her svelte frame and clinging to her hips. Images of her in his king-sized bed fogged his brain. Her long, toned, flexible legs wrapped around his hips, her supple back arched in passion as she rode him, her small, high breasts jutting forward, begging for his mouth. If they were just like any other couple he'd have her in that position pronto.

And why not? She had agreed to marry him. Or, rather, she had acquiesced—because that was what her strained little *For Nadeena* had sounded like to his ears. Even so, he should be feeling relieved right now to have that sorted. Triumphant, even. But he didn't. If anything, he felt as if it was a Pyrrhic victory because, while he might have gained her agreement, he could see by the wall she had erected between them that he had gained very little else.

And right now he wanted to tear that wall down. Right now he wanted more from her than shy, covert glances that only served to heighten his awareness of her as a woman. His awareness of her as *his* woman.

All night she'd been giving them to him as she worked the room like a pro. At first he'd thought her nervousness stemmed from some sort of insecurity but he'd soon discounted that. She'd handled herself beautifully. Talking to the Sultan of

Astiv about his love of antique glassware while those around him nearly fainted with boredom and then recounting war stories about the trials and tribulations of competitive waterskiing with the Prince of Mana.

He'd hated the prince knowing something about her that he hadn't had a clue about and he'd liked even less the way the Prince had looked at her. But then he pretty much didn't like the way any man looked at her and that possessive feeling wasn't something he'd ever had to deal with before.

She gripped her hands together as if she didn't know what to do with them. 'Nadeena is asleep.'

'Good. Maab said she had most of the milk you expressed at eleven o clock.'

'Oh, okay. In that case I'm glad I didn't wake her to change her nappy because she should sleep for a few more hours now.'

'Good.' Nadir wondered how it was he could stand in the middle of the room having a stilted conversation about Nadeena when all he wanted to do was strip Imogen naked and bury himself deep inside her lush body. 'How long do you think we've got before she wakes up?'

He watched her eyes widen as comprehension

dawned and thought, *Oh, yes, my sweet, I have exactly that in mind.*

If he was going to be breaking down walls tonight he didn't plan on doing it with a sledgehammer.

'Not long.'

He smiled. Her 'no' couldn't have been more transparent.

Realising that he still wore his *keffiyeh*, he reached up and yanked it from his head, ruffling his hair. He felt her eyes on him but when he glanced over her gaze flitted away and she shifted like a mare scenting the approach of an overly randy stallion.

She cleared her throat and lifted her chin and he knew she was about to try and call an end to the evening. 'Well, I hope the night was okay from your point of view but—'

'The night was excellent. You were brilliant.'

'Oh. Well, thank you.'

He studied her. 'Why were you nervous tonight?'

'Who said I was nervous?'

He felt a small smile touch his lips. 'I could tell. But I don't know why.'

'Because I knew everyone would be looking at me.'

'But you're a dancer—you must be used to being on show in front of people.'

'Being in a performance is totally different from being myself.'

So he'd been right about the insecurity. He frowned, wanting to reassure her. 'People like you. You're a natural. And a waterskier, I understand. How was it that the Prince of Mana knew that you had once won the Australian championships and I had no idea?'

'Maybe because he asked and you didn't.'

Nadir scowled. 'I'm asking now.'

She shrugged. 'It wasn't that big a deal. My mother was into waterskiing, which is how I came to do it, but when I was sixteen my ballet teacher told me that I needed to give up all dangerous sports if I was to take the dance seriously and I stopped.'

'But you loved it,' he guessed.

Her eyes glowed with an inner light that made them sparkle. 'The speed was pretty exhilarating.'

He grinned. 'Something we have in common.'

In Paris he'd been too obsessed with touching

her to get to know her properly. Now he realised
he wanted both. 'Have a nightcap with me.'

'I don't think that's a good idea.'

Nadir walked over to the wet bar and smiled.
'Have one anyway.'

Imogen knew that smile. He'd used it often when
they'd been out and he'd come up and wrap his
arms around her and tell her something, like how
tired his feet were from walking or how cold he
was and how he really thought they should head
indoors. What he'd meant was that they should
be in bed. Usually she'd melt against him at that
point and he'd hail a cab, her need for him just as
overpowering as his was for her.

Even that first night her need for him had erad-
icated her natural cautiousness around men and
overshadowed her commonsense. She closed her
eyes in the vain hope that the memories would
go away but instead she felt as if she was back in
Paris inside his elegant apartment.

The only reason they'd even shut the main
door that first night was so he could crush her up
against it. After her show he had prowled into the
backstage area, his eyes hot with intent. Imogen
had quivered with raw excitement, a deep femi-

nine instinct having already warned her that he would come for her. And he had. He'd told her his name and asked her how long it would take her to change. When she'd told him ten minutes to scrub off the stage make-up he'd said, 'I'll wait.'

He'd made it sound as if he'd wait for ever. One of the other girls had rushed to lend her a short black dress since she'd only brought her jeans and a T-shirt to change back into and had sighed as if she wished she'd been the chosen one. Heels had materialised and the girls had tittered around her and told her who he was. Imogen hadn't really taken any notice, her mind buzzing with a sexual excitement she'd never felt before. He had taken her to one of Paris's exclusive supper clubs in his black Ferrari and been the perfect gentleman while they ate.

Not that she remembered much of the food. Or the conversation, for that matter, but she remembered how his hands had cradled his glass of Scotch as he'd watched her then he'd led her back to his car, his hand hot on the small of her back. He'd asked if she would like to go to his place for coffee. She'd said yes even though she hated coffee; a fact they had laughed at the following morning.

Imogen remembered feeling immeasurably shy and nervous seeing as how it was her first time going home with a man. Her only other lover had been a self-centred dancer who had come on to her after a sweaty but exhilarating rehearsal in her late teens and the rehearsal had been so much better.

Not that she'd told Nadir any of that. She hadn't known how. To tell him in the car ride to his apartment that she was pretty new to all this would have seemed presumptuous in the extreme and then when they had taken the lift—the very tiny and interminably slow lift—to his floor he hadn't touched her. He hadn't said a word to her in fact and nor had she to him, but her body had hummed with a life of its own and a hollow ache had risen up between her thighs with every floor that flashed past.

Finally they'd arrived. Nadir had pushed the door open, Imogen had made to move past him and accidently brushed her bare arm against his. That was all it had taken. One touch of his skin against hers and she had been lost. Gone up in a fireball of heat and need and powerful yearnings that had driven out all sense and caution. She re-membered that the door had slammed shut and then thankfully she was up against it as her body had grown too heavy for her legs to hold her up.

Nadir had groaned against her neck, told her how much he wanted her. He'd cupped her face and pushed her hair behind her shoulders. Then he'd taken her mouth with his, ran his hands all over her body, pulled up her too-short dress and ripped her silky panties away. Awestruck, Imogen had been unable to do anything but grab onto his broad shoulders and kiss him back as he'd filled her. His body hot and hard and so powerful as he'd thrust into her. She'd had a moment's discomfort, which he'd sensed because he'd slowed and the change in pace had pushed her over the edge em-barrassingly quickly. She'd cried out. He'd cried out and then they had been meshed together, both panting in the silent, dark hallway. He'd given a self-deprecating laugh, told her it had never been like that for him before and carried her into the bedroom. Ran the tub. Made love to her what felt like a hundred times more throughout the night.

'What are you thinking about, *habibi*?' His deep voice broke into her reverie and she started, her hands pleating the sides of her dress.

She took a deep careful breath in and eased it out. She wasn't stupid, she knew what he'd been suggesting before and she knew she wasn't emotionally ready to take that step. Not after a night of having his focus on her as if she was the most important person in the world to him. 'Nothing.'

He stepped in front of her. His eyes were dark and intense on hers. She wanted to look away because she knew her own must mirror the hunger she saw there but she couldn't. She was trapped by a desire that was becoming harder and harder to ignore the more time they spent together.

His eyes slid down her body, warming her from the inside out until they stopped on her hands.

'Where's your ring?'

All night he'd been at her about the ring, telling her not to fidget with it because then everyone would know that it was new.

'Everyone would be right,' she had whispered irritably at the start of the night. 'And it feels wrong on my finger.'

Of course he'd been annoyed by that. 'Before you know it you'll forget it's even there.'

Just as he would one day forget her and Nadeena were even there? 'What did you do with it?' he asked now.

'I took it off,' she said with a touch more defiance than she'd meant.

A muscle ticked in his jaw. 'So you can keep pretending this is not happening, *habibi*?'

When she didn't answer, because yes, in some way it was easier to pretend this wasn't happening, he stalked past her and straight through the doorway into her bedroom.

'Nadir!'

Worried that he would wake the baby, she ran after him and nearly collided with him in the doorway. Grim-faced, he reached for her left hand and jammed the ring back on her finger. 'That stays on.'

Supremely irritated with his overbearing attitude, Imogen wrestled with the ring, not sure what she intended to do with it once she got it off, but Nadir grabbed her hands and shoved them behind her back, bringing her body into full contact with his own.

Time seemed to stop as they stared at each other, both breathing hard. She wanted to tell him to let her go and perversely to hold her tighter at the same time.

She stared up at him, slightly dazed. Perhaps she was losing her mind...

'Dammit, Imogen, you would try the patience of a saint and I'm definitely not a saint.'

She'd had every intention of resisting his kiss but every moment seemed to converge with her wanting his mouth on her. His hands. It was madness. It was glorious and when his mouth came down over hers and his hand rose to palm her breast Imogen moaned and gave herself over to the mindless pleasure of being close to him again. This—touching him, tasting him—was thrilling and she wasn't sure how far she would have gone or when she would have called a halt to things when fate stepped in—or was it luck?—and they both broke apart as the high-pitched wail of a baby's cry rent the air.

Panting and shocked at the sheer wantonness of her own response, Imogen nearly fell out of Nadir's arms in her haste to put some space between them, her mind spinning, her body sluggish with arousal.

Nadir stared at her, his own chest heaving, and beneath his heated gaze and Nadeena's sharp cries her breasts started to tingle and leak milk all over the front of the exquisite silk dress. Mortified, she cupped her hands over her breasts and fled next door to her daughter.

Trying to slow her breathing, she reached for the baby and cradled her against her chest before easing into the corner chair to feed her. 'It's okay, angel. Mummy's here.' She closed her eyes, her face hot with embarrassment at how easily she had slipped back into Nadir's arms without thought or care of the consequences. Yesterday she had been trying to convince him that marriage was a mistake and now she had agreed to it. She had his ring on her finger and she still wasn't sure she wasn't about to make the biggest mistake of her life.

As if conjured by her thoughts, Nadir materialised in the doorway, his hair askew where her fingers had tangled in it, his features drawn tight with unfulfilled desire.

'Do you need anything?' His deep voice rumbled through her and momentarily distracted Nadeena. She glanced down to find her daughter's eyes open and staring, trying to find her father and feed at the same time.

'I'm fine.' Imogen stroked her hand over Nadeena's head, settling her. She wasn't fine, of course—she was flustered, confused, *unsatisfied.*

'Water? Can I get you water?' For the first time he looked out of his depth and her heart clenched. 'I read that breastfeeding mothers need to drink lots of water.'

He had? Her surprise must have shown on her face because he ran a hand through his hair and his jaw set hard.

'Water would be nice,' she said softly, her mind struggling to adapt to the return to normality between them. She shook her head at that. It struggled to adapt to what passed as normality between them since Nadir had stepped back into her life. A normality that was still defined by past hurts and an uncertain future.

'Here.'

She blinked as a glass of water was thrust in front of her.

'Thank you.'

'You're welcome.' He nodded and took it back when she'd drained the glass. 'Can I get you anything else?'

'No, no.' She placed Nadeena on her shoulder to burp her. 'No, everything should be—oh!' Imogen squirmed as she felt warm baby spew slide down over her bare shoulder and the top half of her dress. 'Oh.'

She heard Nadir chuckle. '"Oh" is right.'

The look on his face made her suddenly feel like laughing and groaning at the same time with embarrassment. Then Nadeena grew fussy and started crying, jamming her tiny fists into her mouth.

'What's wrong with her?'

'I suspect it's her teeth.' She touched her hand to Nadeena's forehead. 'She's not overly hot so...' She scrunched her brow. 'It could be that she's just tired and out of sorts because it's late. It's hard to figure out what's wrong with babies sometimes.'

'Not just babies.'

His rueful comment hung between them and just when she might have asked what he meant by it he held out his arms. 'Here, give her to me.'

'No, no...it's fine, I can—'

'I know you can, Imogen,' he agreed flatly. 'But you need to go clean up and I can settle her while you do it.'

'Oh, right.' Clean up. She'd completely forgotten about the sour milk on her shoulder and dress. She handed Nadeena to him and watched as he confidently tucked her into the crook of his muscular arms. 'Come on, *habibti*,' he crooned, 'let's get you settled.'

Again Imogen was momentarily struck dumb by the sight of them together but unfortunately Nadeena didn't stop crying and it made her hurry into the shower, where she quickly rinsed her hair and washed herself.

Pulling on the oversized T-shirt she had used the night before, she hurried back to her room to find Nadir pacing back and forth and singing what sounded like an Arabic lullaby in his soft baritone.

'She's nearly asleep. Should I put her in the cot?'

'I need to change her first.'

'I've done it already.'

Imogen stared at him. 'You have?'

'I'm not completely useless, Imogen. I can change a baby's nappy.'

Given that Nadir was the most capable man she had ever met, she didn't know why she had ever doubted he could. Maybe because her father had never shown much interest in his duties as a parent. It made her realise just how low her expectations had been on the night that Nadir had walked out after discovering that she was pregnant. Maybe they had been low all along.

The thought stunned her.

Had she been waiting for him to disappoint her? Fail her? Because he had. Spectacularly so. Which didn't fit with why he was being so helpful now. Was it to garner her cooperation with his dogged plan for them to marry or because he genuinely cared?

Too many questions and too few answers but Imogen suspected that maybe he wouldn't change his mind about marrying her and, worse, part of her didn't want him to. This…she swallowed back a ball of emotion rising inside her chest…this was nice. Sharing the care of Nadeena with him, working together as a team. It was every woman's wish to have her lover—her partner—around to talk with and iron out the kinks of parenthood. To journey through life hand in hand with someone there to help field the knocks it inevitably handed out. Someone who would care.

But Nadir wasn't her lover or her partner at this point and her mother's dating advice had been to warn her that a man could put on a good show for thirty, even forty, days before the cracks started appearing. If you added up their time together in Paris and the last couple of days, Nadir fell smack bang in the middle of her mother's bell curve. Would he revert to his playboy ways after that and start ignoring them both?

'Imogen?'

Realising she had spaced out and that she was extremely tired after all the emotion of the last couple of days, she glanced up at him holding Nadeena. She looked so tiny and perfect in his arms.

'Just…' She had no idea what she was going to say. 'She might need a top-up.'

'A top-up?'

'A bit more milk.' Her face flooded with colour as he understood and she thought how ridiculous that she should be embarrassed after all they had shared but she was. 'I'll do it in bed. It's sometimes easier.'

'But is it safe? What if you fall asleep?'

'Of course it's safe,' Imogen said sharply. 'I wouldn't put her at risk, Nadir.'

'I wasn't questioning your mothering skills, Imogen, I…oh, hell.' He rubbed his jaw. 'This is all new to me. I want you to be safe.'

Imogen's heart gave a little leap. *Not you*, she derided the foolish muscle in her chest; he means he wants Nadeena to be safe. 'I won't fall asleep,' she said wearily. 'You can go.'

Their eyes connected in the dim light and Imogen saw a look come over his face that she couldn't quite define. If she had to guess she'd say it was as if he was trying to work something out but, whatever it was, it seemed to elude him.

She lay on the bed and waited almost breath-lessly as he leant over and laid Nadeena in the crook of her arm, sleepiness invading her limbs as her daughter latched onto her nipple once again.

'Your hair is wet,' he said gruffly.

'I know.' Imogen lifted her hand to smooth the damp, irritating strands away from her shoulder and tried not to show her surprise when Nadir's hands took over the task, smoothing the long strands out on the pillow behind her.

'It's fine,' she said, her breaths shallow and hurried at the intimacy of the moment. 'You don't have to do that.'

'Stop trying to shut me out, Imogen. If you leave your hair like this it will be all tangled in the morning.'

He continued working out the kinks and Imogen decided it was better if she just let him do it. And it felt good. So good.

'Go to sleep,' he said gruffly as he perched on the bed behind her. 'I'll transfer Nadeena to the cot when she's finished.'

'I can...' Imogen yawned. She wanted to say she could do it but she didn't. Instead she did something she hadn't done for months. She fell into a contented sleep before her baby had fully settled.

CHAPTER TEN

NADIR LOOKED DOWN at the woman sleeping on the bed so soundly, her deep breaths even and relaxed. He remembered that she had always slept like the dead and he had often teased her about how hard he'd had to work to wake her through the night. Sometimes he'd even been in the process of kissing her soft body, teasing her awake with caresses that had tortured him and woken her panting. Always when she came awake like that she had wrapped her arms and legs around him and pulled him closer. Always she had moved with him and he'd angled his body in such a way that he knew would bring her to orgasm in no time. She'd groan in his ear, clasp him tighter, urge him on and then afterwards she'd sigh and curl herself around him, pretty much like she was doing to their daughter right now, and Nadir had the strongest urge to get into bed behind them and do the same thing.

Only he didn't.

They both looked too peaceful. His heart clenched and he took a step back. He wondered how life had brought him to this point. To this woman and child. Fate?

It certainly wasn't planned. All his adult life he'd assumed he'd walk his path alone and he'd been okay with that. After the rigid childhood he'd had where his father's word was law he had made sure that he had plenty of choices in life that had all been about taking care of himself. It was a selfish existence for sure but it was also safe because he didn't need anyone and no one needed him in return.

But that had changed now. Now he had a child and a woman he was responsible for and he was determined that they would make a better family unit than his had been. Nothing would make him turn away from them.

Careful not to wake either female, he carefully lifted Nadeena into his arms and marvelled at how small and how fragile she was. He nuzzled her downy dark hair and breathed in her sweet baby smell.

A smile curved his lips as he recalled how Imogen had tried to put him off marrying her by telling him that babies were smelly. They were but in a good way.

They were also a lot cuter than he'd ever noticed before and he grinned when he placed Nadeena into the cot and she promptly sprawled onto her back with her arms flung out to the sides, her tiny mouth moving as she resettled into sleep.

Feeling comfortable that she wasn't about to wake up, he turned towards Imogen. She had shifted more onto her stomach, her leg hitched high on the bed. If he'd been lying beside her that leg would have been draped over his hips and his groin hardened predictably. He wanted her and he didn't mind admitting it. Sex was normal. Healthy. But deep down he knew what he felt for her went beyond sex. For once he didn't try and stop his mind from drifting back to the way things had been between them in Paris. Carefree and passionate. Relaxed and somehow contented. *Contented?*

His mind processed the thought. Had he really been contented when he'd been with her in Paris? When they'd been strolling together arm in arm around the city just like any other couple in the world? He remembered ignoring those feelings at the time and putting them down to sex. Lust.

Passion. But, looking back, he could see that he'd felt completely at ease in her company. Relaxed and, yes, contented. And then another startling thought gripped him. He didn't want her to endure their marriage. He wanted her to want it. He wanted her to want to make it work as much as he did. He wanted her to want him.

He rubbed his eyes and for the first time he wondered if he was doing the right thing by forcing this marriage onto her. But what else could he do?

She made a sound, almost as if she was having a bad dream, and called out his name. Nadir stilled. In his mind's eye he saw her rising from the bed, her short T-shirt riding high on those shapely legs before she reached him and wound her arms around his neck and pulled his mouth down to hers as she had done so many times in the past.

Naturally enough, she didn't do that but she did call out again and Nadir found himself crossing the floor to her side.

'Imogen?' He reached down and placed his hand lightly on her shoulder. 'You're dreaming, *habibi.*'

He thought he'd spoken softly enough not to really disturb her but her eyes flew open and she blinked and the little frown line appeared as she stared up at him.

'Where am I?'

Despite the warning in his head telling him she was tired and needed sleep, he didn't stop himself from reaching down and placing his finger against the frown line. 'It's okay. You're in Bakaan.'

She made a small sound and pushed up into a sitting position. She wasn't wearing a bra and he couldn't keep his eyes off the gentle sway of her breasts. 'Imogen.' Her name was more like a groan on his lips when he caught her staring at his mouth.

By Allah, he wanted her. Wanted her more than he'd wanted any other woman in his life. More than he'd wanted anything at all for a long time and, as if in slow motion, he reached out and took hold of her hand and tugged her up onto her knees.

She rose to him, all sleepy and pliant, and his mouth swooped down to capture hers in a sweet, lingering kiss. He felt her hands flutter close to his jaw and snag on the stubble of his beard growth. He'd need a shave if he was going to stop himself from marring her pale skin but more than that he needed her and for the first time ever he didn't feel concerned by that driving need.

Something had been slowly changing within him since he'd found her again. He didn't know what it was but it was almost as if a piece of his life had slotted into place. Impossible really, given how out of synch his life was right now but still... the feeling persisted.

Not wanting to disturb Nadeena, he broke their kiss and tugged her towards him. When she clung to his shoulders he swept her into his arms and strode out of the bedroom.

'Nadir?' She wriggled and he let her slide down the length of his body until she found her feet. But he didn't immediately let her go.

'I want to make love to you, Imogen. I want to take you to my bed and show you how well this can work between us. How good it can be again.'

The words were raw, his voice almost hoarse with need. Her eyes widened and even in the low-lit hallway he could see colour rising high on her lovely cheekbones.

She swallowed and pushed the tumble of her hair back from her face and he just wanted to bury his hands in it. He just wanted to kiss her. So he did.

As soon as his mouth touched hers, Imogen felt her body catch fire and soften against him and all thoughts of the past and the future dissolved.

How was it possible to feel so much for one person? To want so much from one person? And then she couldn't think any more. Just feel—her heart ruling her actions.

Moaning, she gripped his hair in her hands, letting her body melt against his. This was what she had craved for so long. This aching pleasure only he could give her. And like this they were equals with no past and no future. Just the present.

Pressing closer, she felt Nadir fall against the wall, his laugh husky as his hungry mouth worked its way down her throat. Imogen arched and rose onto tiptoe, her lower body aching to join with his.

Driven by a deep yearning, she clawed at the yards of fabric that made up his robe and felt him turn them both and press her against the wall, his hands pushing up the hem of her T-shirt and hastily dragging her panties down her legs and then finally, blissfully she felt him cup her and she almost dissolved as he parted her slick flesh and delved between her legs, his fingers and thumb gliding over her and into her and stroking her in all the right places.

'Nadir, you—'

'Imogen, *habibi*, you drive me—'

She shifted and he grunted, wedging his knee

between her thighs to hold her upright while he parted his robes singlehandedly.

Imogen tried to bring her hands down to help him but he effortlessly held her high against the wall, his upper body powerfully hard beneath her fingertips and then he brought her down over the top of him and she heard a loud keening sound as his smooth, thick hardness opened her up and penetrated deep inside her body.

He swore. Maybe she did too and for a minute they were both completely still, suspended between two worlds, both adjusting to the exquisite sensation of being joined together.

Then he tangled one hand in her hair and tugged until her dazed eyes met his. The skin on his face was pulled tight, his eyes glittering with a hunger that sent shivers racing down her spine. Those eyes said that this time together would not be gentle or slow. That it would be fierce and urgent and uncontrolled. That she would feel him plunge into her with every fibre of her being and her body pulsed in anticipation.

'Is this okay?' His question was a panting growl and tinged with desperation as if he was having trouble holding himself back. 'I mean you had a baby not long ago and—'

Imogen wound her legs around his waist and hugged him tight. Now that she had given herself over to this it was all she could do not to let the fire inside burn her up. 'It's fine. Please, Nadir—'

He crashed his mouth down over hers again, his tongue thrusting deep as he gave her what she craved and moved powerfully inside her. In no time at all Imogen felt her orgasm building and writhed against him, forcing him to press one hand against the wall to hold them both upright and then she was there, on the pinnacle of that exquisite release she had only ever experienced in his arms, their mouths fused together as if their lives depended on it. Imogen opened her eyes at that moment to find him watching her and the connection was so elemental it hurtled her over the edge into a place filled with bright lights and dizzying heights. And then it was all too much and she threw her head back and let her release rush through her on long exquisite pulses. Seconds later Nadir's grip on her hips tightened to the point of pain and his thrusts grew brutal just before he threw his own head back and bellowed her name into the still night air.

The comedown from the desperate rush to

orgasm was slow and noisy, both of them panting hard to catch their breaths.

Nadir raised his head from where it was now buried against her neck. 'Are you okay?'

'Yes. Out of shape, but good.'

Nadir gripped the underside of her thighs and hoisted her legs higher around his waist while he remained buried deep inside her. 'You're not out of shape, *habibi*. You're perfect.'

'Where are we going?' she asked quickly as he carried her down the hall.

'My bed.'

'What about Nadeena?'

'I'll leave the door open.' He strode inside the room and didn't even bother with the light as he collapsed with her onto the bed.

Imogen tilted her head back and felt the silky fabric of the comforter against the sensitised skin of her back. Part of her knew that she should get up but her body felt as if it was on fire, renewed desire coiling through every cell, and all she wanted to do was wrap herself around Nadir and not think about anything right now. Not the future that seemed so insurmountable and not the past which was tinged with the bittersweet memories of first love and then the utter despair of rejection. Right now her body just wanted his, *needed* his, and she was powerless to resist.

Not that Nadir was exactly giving her time to question his demands as he kissed and licked his way down over her collarbone towards her breasts.

Before she could object, he raised her T-shirt over her head and tossed it onto the floor.

'This time we do it a little slower,' he said gruffly. 'And I might even throw in a little finesse for good measure.'

Imogen laughed at his playful words and then suddenly felt self-conscious as she realised where his mouth was headed. 'Nadir, stop. My breasts aren't the same any more and I'm feeding.'

He batted her hands away and rose up on one powerful arm to peer down at her, his other hand drawing lazy circles around the outer swells of each breast before cupping each one in turn. She felt her nipples peak and rise up eagerly for his touch. 'I don't care. You're beautiful, Imogen.' He lowered his head and laved one nipple lightly with his tongue, making her gasp with pleasure. Nadir grinned. 'I love that you can feed our child. I love that your nipples are slightly darker than before.' His head bent again and he blew across one straining tip. 'I love your taste. The way you feel.'

Lost in his words and his touch, Imogen's arms rose up again to mould his sinewy shoulders and cling to the taut wall of muscle at his back. It was that untamed, unrefined side of him, encapsulated within sleek, sophisticated masculinity that had always drawn her to him. Had always drawn every woman to him.

Forgetting about the past, she inhaled, pulling the wonderful scent of sweat and man deep into her body. 'I love the way you taste too. Take off your robe. I want to feel you against me.'

Nadir didn't need any further urging and within seconds he had come down over the top of her again. Naked. A gloriously prowling male in his prime. Imogen's breath caught at the sight of his thick length jutting hard up against his ridged abdomen. He was so potently virile. So unselfconsciously male he took her breath away.

'Like what you see, *habibi*?' he drawled lazily.

'*Comme ci, comme ça.*' She pretended to yawn.

He growled at her cheekiness and pushed her thighs wider with his knees. 'I'll give you *comme ci, comme ça*,' he whispered roughly, reaching beneath her to angle her bottom up better for his penetration.

He groaned as he sank into her warm, willing flesh. 'I was going to take this slow but now...' he thrust forward and Imogen clung to his arms, her fingernails digging into his hard biceps to anchor herself against him '...now I just want to plough into you and make you scream. How's that for finesse?'

'Finesse is so terribly overrated.' She gasped out each word as he did exactly what he said.

He grunted his pleasure, his gaze hungry as it raked over her face. 'Tell me if I'm too rough?'

Imogen shook her head and brought her hands up to cup the hard planes of his face, her fingers stroking over the rough bristle on his jaw. 'No. Give me more. I want more.'

'Ah, hell, Imogen. *Habibi.*' His words of praise became more urgent and mixed with Arabic as he drove into her over and over and over until they both fell apart with the extent of another mind-blowing orgasm.

Finally sated, Nadir bent down and kissed her sweetly on the mouth. Then he rolled onto his back and took her with him, tucking her head into the crook of his shoulder and it was as if no time had passed at all. She could almost hear the sounds of Parisians dining and chatting and going about their business from the open window of his apartment. But time had passed and it had created a chasm and her chest tightened as she thought about getting up and going back to her own room. If only she wasn't feeling so weak, ripples of her release still coursing through her lax body.

'What?' he asked as if he sensed her tension.

'I should go back to Nadeena.'

He gently tugged her still damp hair out from under his arm and stroked it back against the pillow. 'Stay. I've missed holding you like this.'

His admission startled her and set off a warm glow as if a cluster of fireflies had set up house inside her chest. 'Me too.'

She felt him place a light kiss against her hair and turned her face into his throat.

'Then sleep. I'll check on Nadeena in a minute.'

She wanted to protest, she wanted to say that she needed to do it because she always had and Nadeena's safety was her responsibility but Nadir rolled her onto her side and spooned her, his big body swamping hers and cocooning her in the most delicious warmth and a deep lassitude invaded her already weakened limbs and turned her limp. It was blissful, this feeling of being utterly taken care of, and no doubt—if she let it— highly addictive.

CHAPTER ELEVEN

OR IT COULD have been highly addictive if it had continued. But of course it had not, Imogen thought glumly as she stretched to place her nose against her knee, her groin muscles protesting the once effortless stretch.

They had made love twice more during the night, once fast and another time slow and indulgent, his fingers drifting and stroking over every inch of her body as if he couldn't get enough of her and then in the morning she'd woken up to find him gone.

At first she'd not minded, stretching her overused muscles and indulging in sensual recall. Then she'd realised that she couldn't hear anything and that she'd overslept for the first time since she'd become pregnant and had raced out of bed, pulling on her T-shirt that had been wedged half under his giant bed and set off down the hallway to find Nadeena's cot empty.

Slightly panicked, she'd then rushed into the living area to find Tasnim and Maab taking care of Nadeena at the outdoor table. Relieved, she'd pulled up, taken her smiling daughter into her arms and hugged her, the rush of relief bringing with it the subtle aches and pains in her body that brought her awareness back to how well loved she had been the night before. Then she'd glanced around for Nadir. Tasnim said that he had given Nadeena the small amount of milk left over from when Imogen had expressed the night before and told them not to wake her unless it was absolutely necessary.

As if on cue, her breasts had tingled and she'd sat in a shaded lounge chair and fed her daughter. And waited for Nadir to return.

She'd sat there with a secret smile on her face and thought that maybe she'd been wrong to leave Paris so hastily fourteen months ago. That maybe she'd been wrong not to have realised that he would want what was best for her and the baby.

That had been yesterday morning's thoughts. Now, another day and a half later, Imogen was wishing that she had run further fourteen months ago and that he'd never found her because, apart from a note sent to inform her that he would be in late last night, she hadn't seen or heard from him since.

It would have been the classical wham-bam-thank-you-ma'am scenario except for the fact that she still had an enormous ring on her finger that she was sure someone would hack off to obtain if she ever ventured out into a public place with it on.

She glanced at it now, wondering why she still wore it.

It wasn't because she was under any illusion that the man who had given it to her genuinely cared about her. And it definitely wasn't because she thought he craved her company as much as she stupidly craved his. Not that he'd ever know that was how she felt. No, she might have felt her heart crack open a little when he was touching her, kissing her, *making love to her,* but his behaviour over the last two days had sealed it back up with more precision than a blowtorch. And to think she'd imagined that she was falling for him all over again. Thank goodness she'd disabused herself of that errant notion.

And yes, on some level she knew she was being unfair to him because of his current issues in Bakaan but she knew he had a reputation for working hard. Working hard and playing hard. So she knew this was just a sign of her life to come and she didn't like it. He made her feel like an afterthought while she found herself wanting so much more from their relationship. More than he clearly did.

The realisation was emotionally debilitating and if he thought that giving her a couple of extraordinary orgasms would be enough to make her comply with his every wish then he had another thing coming. Especially since she'd had at least a day now to stew over the news that they were to be married at the end of the week.

She doubted she would have taken the news that well if it had come from Nadir, but since it had come from Tasnim asking what style of dress she would like to wear she felt like telling Nadir to go to hell. That she'd been right all along and this was nothing but an enormous mistake they would both live to regret.

A slight noise from behind her had her hackles rising as she recognised the subtle shift in the air that told her it was him. Pride kicked in and fortified her spine. There was no way she would let him know that his actions had hurt her. Determined to be cool and dignified despite her racing heartbeat, she finished off a leisurely stretch and then stood up as if she didn't have a care in the world.

He walked towards her, his eyes raking over the casual clothing she had found in amongst the clothes he had provided for her. She hadn't wanted to wear them but then she hadn't really had any choice. Nadir was garbed in traditional white robes that emphasised his regal bearing and sun-bronzed skin. How a man could make robes look sexy was beyond her, but unfortunately they only seemed to enhance Nadir's physical perfection rather than detract from it.

He ran a hand through his hair and she realised that he looked tired beneath his natural tan. 'Where's Nadeena?'

Of course he would ask after their daughter first. It was why she was even here after all. Stupidly, it hurt.

'Having a late afternoon nap.'

He nodded. 'Has she been okay?'

'Great.'

'Okay then it's you.' His eyes narrowed. 'What's wrong?'

She kept her expression bland. 'What could possibly be wrong?'

* * *

Nadir didn't know, but something was. He'd spent the last two days meeting with members of the UAE to determine Bakaan's future membership into the federation and he was exhausted. It had been a frustrating endeavour because his father had never been interested in political or economic alliances and instead had treated Bakaan as a lone wolf. Naturally enough that made some of the members of the federation highly suspicious of what Bakaan's intentions were and what the benefit was in including them into the federation at all. When he had explained his and Zach's vision of the future—drawn up and refined over many years and many lagers—he'd had a breakthrough and all but one had signed the new treaty.

Reform would be slow, he knew, and arduous but intensely satisfying once it started to take effect. And it was also supposed to be Zach's job—not his. Zach, who had still not returned any of his phone calls.

Now Nadir was supposed to travel to Sur, a Northern city, and present the terms of the agreement to the outer tribal elders who still held a lot of influence in certain sectors of Bakaan.

First, though, he'd wanted to stop off and see

Imogen and Nadeena. He'd been frustrated the past two days that he hadn't been able to see them at all but the federation members had been due to leave and Nadir had needed to strike while the iron was hot. When he'd returned to his suite late last night, even though he'd sent a note telling Imogen when he would finish up, he'd been disappointed to find her already in bed. And not his. After their lovemaking two nights ago he'd assumed that things between them would improve. Seeing the look on her face now, he knew that had been an erroneous assumption.

He stepped closer to her and she stepped back. His smile turned wry and he deliberately kept his gaze above her neck or he knew he wouldn't give a damn about finding out what was wrong and fix it in his own way. 'I don't know, Imogen. But something is.'

She shrugged and he gritted his teeth. The wall was back up between them and she'd added a couple of bricks for good measure. Did she really find the idea of being tied to him so hateful? Or was it something else? Her London lover, perhaps?

He tried to cap his instant irritation at the thought of them living together and reminded himself that the buffoon was part of her past and she was as entitled to one as much as he was. Unfortunately, it didn't help. 'Did you get my message last night?'

She tossed her head in a feminine challenge and her wheat-blonde braid swished over her shoulder like the tail of an angry cat. 'I did.'

'But you ignored it.'

'I was tired.'

Not much he could say to that since the reason she was most likely tired was because he'd kept her up most of the previous night making love to her.

'And what would have been the point in waiting up anyway?'

Now there was a lot he could say to that and he barely resisted the urge to just pull her into his arms and show her. 'I would have thought after the night we spent together you wouldn't need to ask that.'

She shrugged again. 'We were two people letting off steam. It meant—'

'Do not say *nothing*, Imogen.' His jaw clenched tight. 'Not unless you want me to set about proving just how much it did mean.'

Her eyes flashed and it looked like she bit her tongue. 'Did you come here for a reason? Has your brother returned?'

He drew his hand across his lower jaw. 'No. Unfortunately not. And something about his lack of contact no longer rings true. I've sent a convoy out to check on his whereabouts. In the meantime I have to convince our tribal leaders in the north that this union will be for the good of Bakaan.'

'Sounds busy. You'd better go.'

A muscle ticked in his jaw.

Imogen turned dismissively as if she had a hundred better things to do and Nadir's frustration and tiredness tripped over into anger. 'You could show a little more interest than that.'

She seemed unconcerned by his outburst. 'What would you like me to say?' She was formal, polite. *Reserved.* The warmth from their lovemaking had gone as if it had never existed. 'Break a leg?'

It took three steps to reach her and when he clamped his hands around her slender arms she went as rigid as a poker. He gentled his touch. 'What's wrong, *habibi*? Has someone upset you?'

She tried to shake him off. 'You don't talk to me about anything—why should I talk to you? I'm just an additional problem you don't want. Nadeena and I both.'

'That's not true. I don't have a lot of time right now.'

'When will you?' She lifted her chin. 'Never, that's when. If this marriage goes ahead—'

'It will.'

'So I heard.' She lifted her chin. 'In five days' time, *apparently*. It would have been nice of you to tell me. What if I wanted to invite some of my friends for support?'

'Invite whomever you want.' His brow furrowed. 'And I thought I had told you. It's been decreed by the council.'

'I don't care if it's been decreed by the Queen of England. The last thing I want is a husband who is off having a good time without his family. I tell you, Nadir, if Nadeena ever hears of any affairs you've had I will unman you.'

'There will be no affairs.'

'Right.' Her green eyes flashed sceptically. 'All that travel and long hours at work...I know how it goes.'

'I do not operate that way and I never have.'

'And if you fall in love one day?' Her delicate brows arched in challenge. 'What then?'

Nadir gritted his teeth. 'That won't happen.'

Instead of being relieved by his reassuring words, she looked achingly vulnerable and he was beyond frustrated because he had no idea how to please her. No idea how to win her over.

'Go away, Nadir. I understand you have important people waiting for you.'

Her words stuck in his head. There was no doubt the emirs waiting for him were important. But so was she and he didn't want to spend another night away from her. 'Actually, I don't. I've cancelled all my other obligations.'

Her eyes narrowed warily. 'You have?'

No, but he would. It was only a white lie and what was he doing telling white lies anyway? He hated lies and liars and had never seen any excuse for those who did so. And yet here he was, telling one because he knew if he didn't he'd somehow hurt her again.

Anyway, Omar could travel north with the emirs. He was equipped for the job and Nadir could use the time to take stock of all that was happening in Bakaan. Take stock of the fact that he'd relished the challenge of the last couple of days. And why wouldn't he? It was what he did for a living after all. Bought companies experts said were dogs and turned them into cash cows.

If it was part of Zach's plan to disappear so that he'd have no choice but to get involved in Bakaani business then it had worked. To a degree because he still wouldn't take on the leadership role, no matter how sly Zach was. But right now all that was second to putting things right with Imogen.

He felt her try to pull away again but he slid his hands down her arms and felt goose bumps rise up on her flesh. His muscles hardened as he registered what the shiver beneath her skin betrayed and the need to stamp his claim on her became paramount. Forcing his hold to remain gentle, he sipped at her lips, took her bottom lip between his teeth and suckled it rhythmically until he heard the small hitch in her breath that said she was his. That little sound always undid him and he drew her closer and groaned as her soft curves yielded to his hardness.

'And I'm taking you out for dinner,' he found himself saying. 'There's a dance troupe in the city showcasing some of Bakaan's tribal dances. They're performing tonight.' He was sure he'd seen it on the list of possible excursions for the emirs because he'd immediately thought of her. 'There might be some other leaders present but I booked a private table.' Another white lie that would only be so until he got onto Staph.

CHAPTER TWELVE

NADIR WAITED FOR Imogen to return from the restaurant bathroom and thought that if one more person stopped at their table to suck up to him he'd have them locked up for making a nuisance of themselves.

Of course it wasn't just him they were interested in. With her blonde hair and natural grace, Imogen would no doubt become the Jackie Kennedy of Bakaan if he were to become King. Something everyone assumed was already the case.

He sighed and was thankfully distracted from heading down that line of thought as Imogen wove her way through the crowd, Bjorn keeping a discreet but alert distance. She'd chosen to wear a traditional *abaya* for their night out and the thoughtfulness of the gesture wasn't lost on him. She could just as easily have worn something shockingly skimpy to embarrass him but it wasn't in her nature. He didn't know why he hadn't seen from the start that she wasn't manipulative or two-faced, as many of the other women he had dated in the past had turned out to be. Women who would simper and preen and bend any which way he asked them to. He smiled as his memories of the other night came back on a rush. He was already looking forward to the end of this evening and bending Imogen to his will again.

'Wow—this looks delicious.'

Nadir followed her gaze to the table. He'd forgotten all about the food.

'I hope you didn't wait for me to start.'

'Of course I did.'

'Oh, thanks.' She leant forward and sniffed appreciatively. Her eyes closed and a look of total bliss swept across her face and he very nearly called for his car.

'Is that cardamom and cinnamon I can smell?'

'And vanilla and honey,' he said roughly. Like her skin.

'What's this dish?'

Shelving his sexual appetites for now, Nadir turned his attention to the food. For the next hour they ate and talked and when it was time for the music to start the tables were cleared to make room for the dancers to take the floor. Of course he and Imogen were given a central position and moments later a lute started playing. Then a flute joined in along with a *riqq*. Imogen started swaying in time with the music.

She leant closer to him so that she could be heard above the music and revelry of the excited audience, her lips so close to his ear he could feel her warm breath. 'What's that instrument?'

Nadir turned his head, his gaze snagging with hers, their mouths inches apart. He thought about kissing her but knew he couldn't. Public displays of affection were currently considered a crime in Bakaan. Instead he inhaled her fragrance and reminded himself that he was a man reputed to have wonderful self-control. 'Which one?'

She swivelled her head and pointed towards a group of musicians and he breathed in her tantalising scent.

'The one across that man's lap that looks like a harp.'

'A *qanun.*'

She smiled up at him. 'It's beautiful.'

No, she was beautiful and he wondered how it was possible for his heart to feel so light when Zach's continued lack of contact was starting to worry him and insurgents were right now threatening to disrupt industry in the north.

She tapped her feet in time with the music and the lead dancer noticed. With a smile on her face she headed their way and Nadir knew what was coming.

'Would the new Sheikha like to join in the line-up?'

Imogen's face lit up and she said, *'Shukran,'* which impressed everyone within earshot, and joined them.

The audience cheered when they realised what was going on and the female dancers surrounded Imogen, much to Bjorn's consternation, and wound shimmering skeins of fabric around her to match their own costumes.

She stood with her feet together, toes turned out and he grinned as he remembered the time he had teased her about looking like a duck. She'd quacked and told him that after years of dancing she couldn't help it. He'd kissed her and told her he loved it. He still did.

Missing a step, she laughed and delighted the other dancers with her unaffected nature and he tensed as he wondered how any man looking at her could fail to want her as much as he did.

Immediately following that thought was the one that said he should bundle her up right now and take her back to the palace. Back to his bed.

Only the dance had started and he couldn't turn away from her as she mastered the routine. His gut tightened and then the dance changed and the men joined in.

They looked at him with an air of hope rather than expectancy because, of course, his father had never mixed with his people like this, preferring to rule from the lofty heights of the palace walls. If he were to take the job he wouldn't rule that way and neither would Zach.

And then he realised what dance they were about to perform. It was the dance a man did when he was courting a woman and his instinct was to beg off but then he caught Imogen's eyes, her swaying figure. To hell with it. He moved to stand opposite her. He had never performed it before but he had seen it done many times as a boy. She looked up at him with a shy expression. Did she know what this performance represented? That it signified undying love?

His steps faltered as he circled her. Was that what he was feeling? Love? He immediately dis-carded the idea. He'd never wanted to find love in his life because—as he'd learned from first-hand experience—deep emotion brought even deeper mistakes and he liked his mind clear and sharp. Not that it was exactly clear or sharp right now but that was just lust and lust could be sated.

Imogen's words about how she only wanted to marry for love came back to him. What would it be like to have hers? Something tightened in his chest. He didn't want that from her. It was enough that they were compatible in bed. That they enjoyed each other's company. He stepped closer to her than he should have. 'Let's get out of here,' he growled in her ear.

She looked up at him with big eyes and he thought to hell with it and kissed her before dragging her off the dance floor amidst the shocked gasps of his countrymen. Things would be changing soon enough in Bakaan. He'd just add PDAs to that long list of improvements.

Imogen could feel the tension radiating from Nadir's big body in the car and desire made her blood grow sluggish in her veins. That dance they had performed back at the restaurant had been highly erotic even though they'd never actually touched. And Nadir had performed it like a professional.

She'd guessed that it was some sort of mating ritual and she wondered if Nadir had ever danced it with another woman before. She wanted to ask, but she wouldn't.

Instead she thought about how much his people had loved it when he'd joined in and she wondered yet again why he didn't want to be King. He would be exceptional in the role. Was it because of his father? His sister who she didn't feel comfortable enough asking him about? And when would she start to feel comfortable enough with him to be able to freely discuss what was on her mind?

'Did you have a good time?'

'Yes.'

His eyes narrowed. 'You're biting your bottom lip. What's wrong?'

Imogen glanced at the driver of the car. 'Nothing.'

'By now I understand that *nothing* inevitably meant *something.*'

'You're not that clever,' she said, smiling in spite of her misgivings. But he was and it was a bit disconcerting to think that he knew her so well already.

Fortunately he let it drop as the car swung through the palace gates and stopped at the front steps. They both got out and Nadir didn't try to talk to her until he'd closed the door to his suite.

After finding out Nadeena was okay, Imogen once again found herself standing awkwardly before Nadir when what she'd love to do was go up to him and wrap her arms around his neck and kiss him.

With masculine grace he moved to lounge on the sectional sofa. 'You want to talk about nothing yet?'

Imogen sighed. 'Okay, fine. I was wondering why it is you don't want to be the next leader of Bakaan.'

She saw the minute the shutters came down over his eyes and shook her head. 'And why it is that as soon as I ask you something personal you refuse to talk.'

'I run a large organisation that is already showing the strains of my absence. I don't have time to run Bakaan as well.'

'You told me once that you love to take companies that are on the verge of collapse and turn them into something wonderful and, from what I can tell, Bakaan is in an identical situation.' She studied the way he rigidly held himself. 'If it helps, you are clearly a natural born leader, Nadir, and the people love you. You could do this job with your eyes closed.'

'It's not a question of capability. It's...' He sprang from the sofa as if he had too much energy coursing through his system. 'I never expected to do it. And what about you? That would make you my queen. Given that you're struggling with the whole concept of wife I can't imagine you'd be thrilled with the role.'

Surprised that he was even asking for her opinion, Imogen thought carefully before answering. 'I honestly don't know. I always thought I would one day open a dance studio and teach dance and... women seem to be very much held back here.'

'In some ways, yes, but equal opportunity for women is one of the key reforms Zach and I have discussed, along with better social infrastructure that would turn Bakaan into a competitive and vibrant place people would want to visit and invest in.' He stopped as if he realised how impassioned he sounded. 'Zach will make a great leader. And you should definitely open a studio. You're a beautiful dancer.'

Was he serious?

'You'd accept having a wife who danced for a living?'

'Why not?'

'I don't know...' Imogen felt at a loss. 'Maybe because you're a prince who has a Harvard education and speaks nine languages.'

The way he studied her unnerved her. 'Why should that matter?'

'I don't know but it does.'

'Not to me.' He frowned. 'Who made you feel bad about your profession? About yourself? Was it your father?'

His shrewd comment startled her. 'Why would you say that?'

'My head of security spoke with him when I was trying to find you and, as far as I'm concerned, a man who doesn't know the whereabouts of his daughter can't be much of a father.'

'He wasn't. And no, he never approved of my occupation. He was quite tyrannical at times and really remote at others. It was very confusing when I was little.'

'Ah, don't tell me—his affection was conditional on how well you toed the line.'

'Your father too?'

Nadir raised an eyebrow. 'My father's idea of giving someone a choice was to tell them how he wanted it.' A shadow came across his face as clear as a puff of smoke being brought in on the breeze. 'I left home at fifteen and headed to the Caribbean, where I took up bartending at a strip club.'

Her eyes widened with shock. 'You did not!'

He laughed. 'I can mix a Slow, Comfortable Screw with the best of them, I promise.'

'Nadir!' Imogen covered her mouth to stop a giggle from breaking out. 'Seriously?'

'It wasn't the most salubrious establishment on the street. After that I joined a building crew in the States and made money playing online poker.'

'I...I'm shocked.' And he made her Moulin Rouge career look like Disney. 'I take it you and your father weren't close,' she said ruefully.

'Actually, we were in the beginning. I was the heir. The golden child. As far as my father was concerned I could do no wrong.' He paused and stared into the middle distance for so long she started to think he'd finished but he hadn't. 'And then I did.'

His blue-grey gaze fixed on hers as if challenging her to ask him what he'd done that was so bad he'd lost the position as the favourite son, his face a mask of dark shadows.

The moment seemed distinctly brittle compared to their earlier camaraderie and she didn't know what to say. Ever since he'd come back into her life she'd wanted him to open up to her like this and share more of himself but now she felt that it would be invasive to ask him to continue because it was obvious these memories were incredibly painful.

He regarded her from beneath his long lashes, a look of self-disgust etched across his face. 'You don't want to know what I did?'

The quietly spoken question was savage and underscored by deep pain. Imogen swallowed heavily. She wanted to go to him and offer comfort but she had no idea how he'd respond to that kind of overture other than to disconnect from her again and it pained her to feel so awkward at a time when she felt he needed her the most. 'Only if you want to tell me,' she said, deciding that the decision had to be his alone without any real prompting from her.

He scrubbed a hand across his face in a gesture she knew meant that he was stressed and her heart went out to him.

'If we stay here for any length of time you'll find out anyway.' The words were toneless, as if he'd locked all emotion about what he was about to reveal in a place he could no longer access.

'When I was fifteen my mother and twin sister were killed in a car accident because my father's soldiers were chasing after them.'

His twin sister?

'Oh, Nadir, that's horrible.' She knew words were inadequate in the face of losing someone special because she still remembered how it had felt to lose her mother but she said it anyway because she wanted him to know that she was there for him. 'Why would they do that?'

'My sister suffered from Tourette's syndrome and my father never accepted her condition.' His tone was layered with resentment and contempt. 'As she got older my mother saw how detrimental life was for her in Bakaan and she wanted to move to somewhere in Europe.' His expression hardened. 'My father refused her request even though they were divorced and so she decided to do it in secret. I was supposed to go with them but I knew my father would be angry and I didn't trust what he would do once he found out.'

Almost afraid to ask the obvious question, she did anyway. 'And did you? Go with them?'

He walked away from her towards the windows and leant his arms against the frame as he gazed out at the darkness. 'No.'

If Imogen had ever heard a more bleak word she couldn't remember it and she waited for him to continue, suspecting that whatever he revealed next cut right to the core of who he was as a man. 'Selfishly, I didn't want them to leave either and so I told my father the plan.' He gave a brittle laugh. 'He set his men onto them; my mother panicked during the chase and rolled the car down a steep incline. They died instantly, so I was told. A small comfort, wouldn't you say?'

Imogen sat so perfectly still she wasn't even breathing—she didn't know what to say. It was clear that he blamed himself for their accident and she wasn't sure words alone would be sufficient to ever relieve his guilt. And in a way she understood how he felt because she was sure if their situations were reversed she'd feel just as awful as he did about it. But she also knew that he had to deal with his guilt and let it go because it really hadn't been his fault.

She remembered what he'd said to her on her first night at the palace about how his parents had dragged him and his sister through their marital problems and suddenly she saw him as the eldest child who had been torn between his love and loyalty to both parents and who was damned if he did and damned if he didn't. At least in her own situation she'd had her mother's unconditional love. Nadir had only had his brother...and his sister, who he no doubt felt he had to protect and whose life he felt he had cut short, and she could only imagine how horrible he must feel.

Wanting to at least close the physical distance between them, she went to stand beside him. She stared at his austere profile and she knew she had tears in her eyes because she just felt for him so much and wanted to rip the pain from his body with her bare hands.

'Afterwards my father refused to give either one of them an honourable funeral.'

Imogen's brow scrunched as she absorbed that piece of information. She shook her head. 'Why not?'

Nadir sucked in a deep breath and she knew he was containing his emotions and locking them down tight. 'He said that they had dishonoured and disrespected him and so to this day they don't have headstones on their graves.'

Without thinking, she reached out and covered the hand he rested on the windowsill with her own. His was much larger than hers and sprinkled with dark hair that stroked across her senses.

It also felt cold. 'Was that why you left Bakaan when you were fifteen?'

'Yes.' He watched her fingers lightly stroke over the back of his knuckles. 'We argued about it and because I had challenged him once too often he disowned me so I left.'

And closed himself off from everyone ever since. 'Nadir, you know you can't blame yourself for what happened. You were only a child.'

He carefully shifted his hand out from underneath hers. 'I was fifteen. Old enough to know better,' he said bitterly.

'No, not old enough to know better,' she denied hotly and she knew that first-hand because at fifteen she had witnessed her father's affair with another woman and she'd had no idea what to do about it. In the end she hadn't told her mother because she'd known it would break her heart but her father assumed that she had and it had led to him leaving anyway.

He moved away from her and she heard the give of the cushions as he dropped back onto the sofa.

'I don't even know why I told you any of that so please if you're going to patronise me by trying to make me feel better then don't. Nothing will ever do that.'

Imogen crossed to stand behind the opposite sofa and gripped the backrest. 'I'm not being patronising, Nadir, but it's not rational to think that you caused their deaths.'

'I was a selfish idiot.'

'You were a *normal* teenager who was trying to keep his world intact.'

'Imogen—'

'No, I'm serious. I know you're hurting over this but how long are you going to punish yourself for the actions of a man who was an adult and should have behaved better?'

'You don't understand—I knew he would go after them.' His voice sounded as if it was wrenched from a place that was deep and dark.

Rounding the sofa, Imogen stopped directly in front of him. 'Nadir, you loved them and it sounds like your loyalty was completely divided. That's not a nice thing for parents to do to kids of any age.'

'There's no excuse for selfishness.'

'Maybe it wasn't you who was the selfish one. Maybe it was your parents.'

He looked at her as if he'd never contemplated that before and she knew that was probably because instead of processing what had happened he'd just tried to completely forget about it. 'Did you happen to get counselling at all?'

Her question brought a surprised bark of laughter. 'Sure I did. The place was called The Painted Pony.'

Imogen put her hands on her hips and felt the air between them become charged as his gaze drifted over her. 'I'm not talking about the strip place you worked at, although I'm sure there were many ladies ready to offer you a shoulder to cry on.'

'Unfortunately, I don't cry.'

'What a surprise. But, seriously, Nadir. I hate to think that you still blame yourself for something that really wasn't your fault.'

'And I hate to think that we're going to waste a whole evening while Nadeena is asleep rehashing an event that is best forgotten.'

Deciding to ignore that, she continued as if he hadn't spoken. 'Tell me this,' she began quietly. 'If this was Nadeena and she had made a mistake like the one you feel you made would you want her to punish herself for it for ever?'

He pushed himself up from the sofa and paced away from her, holding himself rigid. 'That's unfair.'

The fact that he'd even shared this side of himself with her made Imogen glow. It meant that he trusted her. And maybe it was time for her to start trusting him a little as well. 'Maybe you're the one who is being unfair. To yourself.'

Without thinking too much about it, she went to him and wrapped her arms around his broad back.

He stiffened but didn't move away from her and she could feel the heat of his body through the thin cotton of his *dish-dasha*. 'I think your mother and sister want you to be happy, don't you?'

He made a low sound in his throat that sounded like it came from a wounded animal and her heart felt as if it had been squeezed by a giant fist.

Acting purely on instinct, she ran her hands across his broad shoulders and pressed herself closer. He didn't move a muscle but she knew she'd got to him because his breathing quickened just a little. Circling around, she stopped directly in front of him and smoothed her hands over his chest.

Emboldened by the fierce glitter in his eyes, she reached up and pulled his head down to hers. He yielded but she knew his mind was still in another place. A bad place.

About to pull back and give him time, she groaned with pleasure as he plunged his hands into her hair and took her mouth in a hungry kiss that completely immobilised her. Dazed at the swift rise of arousal, she pulled at his robe and moaned in frustration when she could find no way into it. 'These things are not fashioned for easy access, are they?' she complained.

Nadir growled and reefed the garment over his head and she heard one of the seams give in his haste to get it off.

Trembling with excitement, Imogen dug her fingers into the waistband of the cotton pants he habitually wore beneath the *dish-dasha* but his hands shoved hers out of the way so he could pull at her own clothing.

Hampered by the delicate *khaleeji abaya* she had chosen, he cursed in Arabic and she gasped when he grabbed hold of the neckline and ripped it clean down the middle. With her breasts bared to his gaze and his hands, Imogen felt her nipples peak as he bent his head to take one into his mouth. She threaded her fingers through his hair to hold him tight and felt his own skim down over her quivering belly, sucking in a deep breath as he ran the tips of his fingers around the lace between her legs.

'So wet,' he murmured. Imogen moved against

him but his hands drifted to her thighs, gripping her hips as he dropped to his knees and kissed a line down her belly.

'Nadir, I—'

She didn't finish her sentence because he hooked his fingers inside her panties to remove them and widened her stance with one hand while he delved between her legs with the other. Almost sobbing with need, Imogen placed her hands on his shoulders and watched as he pressed his face between her legs and stroked her with his tongue. She cried out as he pleasured her, her long hair swinging around them like a curtain as she almost bent double when her orgasm hit.

'Imogen.' Nadir lifted his head and scattered kisses across her pelvis. 'Your taste drives me wild.'

Gazing down at him with his knees spread wide on the carpet and his chest bare, Imogen swooned. 'I want to taste you too.'

She dropped to her knees as he rose before her and shoved the soft cotton pants down his legs. As always the sight of him aroused and erect gave her pause because he was just so big and imposing, so lethally male.

'Touch me, *habibi*,' he urged in a raw voice

husky with need, his hands tangled in her hair, his warm strong fingers massaging her scalp. So she did. Flicking her tongue out to wrap around the head of his shaft as her hands slid rhythmically up and down. He let her have her way with him for what seemed like only seconds before he took over, groaning about self-control and need as he pushed her to the floor. Then he was above her and the only sounds that broke the silence were the mingling of their own harsh breaths.

'Look at me, *habibi*,' he commanded. 'I love to watch your eyes as I come inside you.'

'Nadir, please—' Imogen threw back her head as he shifted his weight and then drove deeply into her slick heat. She couldn't have said if her eyes were open or closed because she was in another world and when he brought his mouth down on hers in a demanding kiss she could hold nothing back as her world coalesced into this moment and then splintered into a trillion tiny pieces. He swore and Imogen held his head in her hands and wound her tongue around his as her orgasm continued to roll through her.

Unable to contain his own climax, Nadir threw back his head and roared his own relief and Imogen knew she would do anything for this man.

That she would follow him anywhere. That she loved him completely and utterly.

God, did she? Had she really fallen for him all over again? No, she hadn't fallen all over again because she'd never stopped loving him. She groaned and didn't realise she'd made the sound out loud until Nadir swiftly rolled to the side so he was no longer covering her. 'Are you okay?'

Cold replaced his slick warm skin and she shivered. *Was she okay? Would she ever be again?*

'Imogen, did I hurt you?'

No, not yet. 'No.' She cleared her throat and shifted on the silk Persian carpet beneath her. 'I'm fine.' At least she hoped she was.

He leaned over and cradled her cheek in the palm of his hand. 'You're sure? I wasn't too rough?'

God, he was divine. Beautifully rugged and so elementally male. Would he hurt her? Or did knowing that he would never love her mean that he didn't have that power any more? Because it was the hope before that had made the crash-landing so disastrous, wasn't it?

'Imogen, you're scaring me.'

'I'm sorry. I'm fine. I was just thinking…I was thinking that this thing…'

She fluttered her hands between them and he smiled. 'It only gets better. Stronger.'

Was he feeling it too? Was it possible he had fallen for her as well? 'Yes,' she whispered, her heart lodged somewhere near her throat and constricted her breathing. 'I...'

'Yes,' he agreed and pushed her hair back from her face. 'Every time we make love I want you more. I wouldn't have said that was possible. It's certainly never happened to me before.'

'Possible...' And then his meaning became clear and she felt quite ill. 'Sex?' He was talking about sex...

'Not just sex.' His eyebrow rose in a sexy slant. 'Hot sex.' He kissed her. 'Great sex.' Another kiss. *'Phenomenal* sex.' His smile was sinful and Imogen buried her face against his neck.

God, she had nearly made an utter fool of herself by blurting out what was in her heart and he was talking about sex!

'I've made you blush.'

She forced herself to laugh softly because what else could she do?

'You feel the same.' There was a deep satisfaction in his voice and Imogen pushed her feelings aside. She raised a small smile because she knew this wasn't a love match and to his credit he had never pretended it was. And what would telling him how she felt achieve anyway? It would only make her feel awkward around him and probably him around her as well.

No, it was better if this was her secret to deal with alone.

CHAPTER THIRTEEN

IMOGEN CAME AWAKE slowly and felt the sun on her face before she opened her eyes. She felt blissfully relaxed right up until she realised that she was alone in Nadir's bedroom; the only sound she could hear was a hawk calling periodically outside her window.

Nadir had gone again. He'd woken early and left her. Still unused to having help with Nadeena, she sprinted out of bed and only paused long enough to pull on a robe behind the door on her way out. It was Nadir's robe, of course, and it smelt of his special blend of male and spice. Trying to ignore the way his scent made her tingle all over, she padded quickly down the marble hallway and into the living room.

When that was empty she headed for the outdoor terrace.

Expecting that she would find the same scene as she had the last time, Imogen heard the sound of Nadeena's infectious giggles. She waited for the sight of the devoted Maab playing peekaboo with Nadeena when her heart all but flew into her mouth as she discovered that it wasn't Maab or Tasnim entertaining her daughter, but Nadir—in the pool. The sight of his bronzed torso stopped her in her tracks and she drooled at the way the sun glinted off his skin and turned it to burnished copper.

Pausing in the doorway and half hidden by a massive potted palm, Imogen watched Nadir throwing Nadeena up in the air and catching her just as her toes flittered across the top of the water, his biceps stretching and bulging in a fascinating display while Nadeena squealed with delight and clung to his neck.

She watched quietly for a moment, completely unnoticed as father and daughter frolicked in the sunshine. It seemed impossible that only a few days ago he had been a single-minded playboy who worked and played to excess and she could hardly fathom that he could be just as at home presiding over a boardroom full of world leaders as he was blowing raspberries on a baby's stomach.

His handling of Nadeena as he turned her onto her stomach and floated her across the top of the water, speaking to her softly in his native tongue was gentle and tender. But then she'd always known he had the capacity for that because she'd experienced it herself fifteen months ago in Paris.

And after last night she knew he was a man who felt things deeply and she felt awful. Awful for the tragedy he had endured and for the fact that he believed he had created it and awful because she had kept Nadeena's birth from him and had never planned to tell him. In her defence, she had believed that she was acting in the best interests of her daughter but watching the two of them together over the past few days had shown her that she had been wrong.

It seemed bizarre that a week ago she would have said that he was not father material and yet her own father had been held up as a wonderful family man in the community and she didn't have one memory of him holding her and playing with her as Nadir was doing with their baby now.

A lump formed in her throat. Yes, Minh had played with Nadeena and there was no doubt he was a wonderful male figure whom she hoped would stay in their lives for ever but he wasn't Nadeena's flesh and blood and why would she want to substitute that when Nadir obviously cared for their baby so much already? Yes, he could change his mind one day; yes, he could walk away, but maybe he wouldn't either.

'Imogen! *Habibi.*'

Catching sight of her, Nadir moved towards the edge of the pool and Nadeena bounced in his arms with excitement as she smiled and stepped outside. 'I've been teaching the kid to swim and she's a natural.'

Imogen grinned as he called her *the kid.* 'She's five months old—you can't possibly tell.'

'I can tell. And I read that the earlier you get a child used to water the better they are and she loves it.'

She also loved him, by the look of glee on her chubby face, and it only drove her feeling of guilt deeper. 'Does she need feeding?'

'Maybe.' His gaze swept over her and she realised how dishevelled she looked. 'You come straight from bed, *habibi*?'

The way he said *bed* made her blush and she was constantly surprised by her visceral reaction to this man. All he had to do was look at her like he was now and she would happily let him do whatever he wanted as frequently as he wanted. Was it any wonder she had fallen for him again?

She knew she'd been a fool to think that she could spend time with someone so utterly virile and not crave more.

'Are you hungry?' he said, climbing out of the pool with Nadeena lifted high against his shoulder. 'There's pastries and fresh fruit on the table and also a pot of tea, although it might need reheating.'

'Thanks.' About to take Nadeena from him, she was startled when he dropped a sweet lingering kiss on her lips. '*Sabah el kheer.* Good morning, beautiful,' he said with a sexy grin.

Imogen swallowed the lump that hadn't quite disappeared from her throat. 'Good morning to you too.'

She settled into an outdoor chair and put Nadeena to her breast while Nadir sat beside them and fielded calls on his phone. He hadn't bothered to put anything else on in the heat and she couldn't take her eyes off his long lean form in black swimming trunks and nothing else.

When Nadeena had finished he made a joke about her burping technique and walked Nadeena around until her stomach had settled.

Knowing there was no easy way to say what needed to be said, Imogen decided to just bite the bullet. 'Nadir, I'm sorry I didn't try to contact you when she was born. It was wrong of me. I see that now.'

Nadir stilled as if he hadn't been expecting her apology and why would he? It was only this morning she'd really understood how wrong she had been.

He looked at her. 'I wasn't exactly at my best at the time I found out you were pregnant.' He rubbed his stubbled jaw and gave her a crooked grin. 'And I don't blame you at all for running when you did. Hell, I probably would have as well.'

Imogen hated that he still thought she had run from him but then she realised with a flash of insight that that was exactly what she had done.

She had run.

She had done what she had so often begged her mother to do when she'd found her crying over her father yet again.

'That's nice of you but in hindsight I should have hung around to have at least talked to you.'

'But I wasn't there, *habibi*, and I didn't tell you when I'd be coming back.'

She sighed. 'I know, but...'

He moved closer to her and slipped the arm not

holding their daughter around her waist. 'It's I who owe you an apology, Imogen. I was the one who failed you in your time of need.'

'No...' She shook her head and he leaned in and kissed her. Nadeena clapped her hands and Imogen's smile turned watery.

'Yes.' His voice was rough with emotion. 'I should not have walked out on you. It was cowardly.'

'You were in shock.'

'So must you have been.'

Imogen bit her lip and studied him. 'You don't think I did it deliberately, do you? You don't think I tried to trap you?'

He shook his head. 'At first I thought all types of things like that. But I don't any more. I know you would never do something like that.'

Imogen smiled, wondering how it was that she felt better when she'd wanted to make him feel that way.

'What was her birth like?'

His gruff question surprised her and it took her mind back to what might just be the best and toughest day of her life. 'It was hard,' she admitted. 'I was in labour for twenty-four hours and...

well, you've probably heard women talk about pushing out a watermelon?'

Nadir nodded.

'Try a beach ball.' She laughed and picked up a bottle of water from the table and took a gulp. 'A very large and very hard beach ball.' Her eyes misted over. 'And then it was over and she was on my chest and honestly I…' Her throat clogged as she remembered that she had looked around the stark, empty hospital room and wished that Nadir was there. She could feel the heat of his gaze on her and her eyes caught his. 'The midwife said that during the birth I called your name.'

In the process of laying Nadeena on a shaded rug, he stilled and looked at her. Imogen instantly felt self-conscious revealing so much and would have taken another quick gulp of water but Nadir was there and pulling her in against his chest. 'I'm so sorry I let you down.' He drew back and stared into her eyes. Rubbed his thumb gently over the drop of water that clung to her lower lip. 'I'm so sorry you had to go through that alone.'

'I wasn't completely alone.' She sniffed back a rush of tears. 'Minh visited and took care of us afterwards.'

'Great.' The word came out on a snarl. 'Remind me to thank him next time I see him.'

Wondering what was up with him, she frowned. 'He's com—'

Nadir placed a finger over her lips. 'I don't want to talk about him.' His voice was low and fierce. 'You won't ever need him or any other man again, do you understand, Imogen?' He was as intense as he had been when he'd told her he was taking her to Bakaan and wouldn't accept any arguments and Imogen was riveted. 'And if we have more children you will never have to go through that without me again. I promise.'

More children? She hadn't given any thought to more children but they hadn't used contraception the whole time they had been in Bakaan. Silly, but she hadn't even thought of it. Her hand went to her belly and she tried to make sense of the jumbled emotions that assailed her. Happiness, disbelief, anxiety...

'What is it, *habibi?* Don't you want more children?'

Yes, oh, yes. She loved being a mother. 'Yes. Do you?'

His smile was the sweetest thing Imogen had ever seen. 'Many.'

A giddy thrill rushed through her. The only thing that would make this moment more special was if he said that he loved her.

She let out a shaky breath. Oh, what she would give to hear those sweet words come out of his mouth.

'I never thought you wanted children,' she said softly.

He gave a short laugh. 'I didn't. I guess things change. People change.'

Imogen thought about her father and wondered if he had changed. If he was nicer to his new family. Had it just been her and her mother he couldn't love?

'What is it, *habibi*?'

Imogen bit the inside of her lip. She smiled up at him and shook her head. 'Nothing.' Why ruin the moment by thinking about the past? Nadir cared about her, she could see that much in his eyes, and he wanted her. Physically, their relationship was as good as she could wish for. As good as she remembered. She rested her head against his shoulder and tried not to give in to the gremlins inside her head that said this bubble of happiness couldn't last.

'Come—I have organised a surprise.'

'What is it?'

'Sand-boarding.'

Having expected him to say something like spa, or oasis, or beach, Imogen was completely flummoxed when he named something she'd never heard of before and which sounded like something builders did to houses when they repaired them. 'What is it?'

'You'll love it, *habibi*. Trust me. It's just like waterskiing.'

'I trusted you,' she groaned as she stretched her over-worked hamstrings. 'And sand-boarding is nothing like waterskiing.'

Nadir lounged in the doorway to her bedroom and grinned. 'It isn't?'

Imogen glared at him. Sand-boarding had been just part of the surprise he had organised. He'd also taken them to an oasis and taken delicious advantage of their time alone together every time Nadeena went down for a nap. They had existed in a blissful bubble and then she'd ruined it by trying to sand-board down a dune as big as a mountain. 'You know it isn't. It's completely insane to throw yourself down a one hundred foot sand dune in the middle of the blazing sun.'

'Ah, but that was your mistake, *habibi*—throwing yourself down. The trick is to actually stay on the board.'

Imogen rubbed her sore bottom she'd used to skate down when the steep incline had petrified her. 'Thanks for the tip.'

'But I was very impressed that you even tried it. I don't know another woman who would.'

Imogen rolled her eyes because she'd slid most of the way down on her bottom. 'Pride,' she said ruefully. 'They say it always comes before a fall and I fell so often my butt is still stinging.

Nadir straightened away from the door and came towards her. 'I can kiss it better if you'd like?' He leaned in and kissed her and Imogen wrapped her arms around his neck. Finally when he drew back he left his arms around her waist and she gazed up at him. 'I've had a wonderful couple of days. Thank you.'

'My pleasure. I hope you enjoyed the oasis. It's one of my favourite spots.'

'It was extraordinary and I don't know why it isn't already on everyone's top ten tourist destinations. Really, Nadir, your ideas for turning it into an eco-resort are second to none.'

'You are second to none, *habibi*. Now, please tell

me you have changed your mind about us spending the night before our wedding alone.'

Imogen pulled back and made a face. 'I haven't. You know it's a tradition for the bride and groom to spend the evening apart and I want to start our marriage off on the right foot.' And usually the bride spent it with her friends but Caro and Minh hadn't been able to fly in until tomorrow so it was just going to be her and Nadeena once Nadir left. 'But what about Zachim? I know you're really worried about him now and if you want to postpone the wedding we can.'

'No.' He shook his head. 'The council have turned it into a big deal so it's important that our wedding goes ahead. I'll find Zach.'

'And if you don't?'

'I will.'

He was always so confident. So sure.

'Tell me, are you happy, *habibi*?'

Imogen hesitated. Would she jinx herself by saying yes? Because she was happy. Happier than she had been in a long time. Deciding that was a silly superstition anyway, she nodded. 'Yes, I am.'

He kissed the tip of her nose and went to the cot to kiss his daughter, who lay sprawled asleep on her back, and Imogen wrapped her arms around herself and wondered if she had a right to feel so contented.

'Goodnight.'

Nadir gave her a searing kiss that nearly had her changing her mind about tradition but then he pulled away, briefly rested his forehead against hers and left.

Imogen closed the door behind him and leant against it, which was when she realised that she was still wearing his *keffiyah*.

Pulling it from her head, she clutched it to her chest as she remembered him winding it around her head to keep the sun from burning her. She sighed. Already she felt lonely without him and she told herself it was dangerous to want him so much. Dangerous to rely on him so much. But, try as she might, she couldn't remove the grin from her face.

Her phone beeped a text message and she smiled when she saw it was from Minh, telling her they would be arriving tomorrow around noon. Since the wedding wasn't until the afternoon, that would give them time to catch up beforehand.

When she had invited them she had been feeling as if her world was crashing down around her and she'd desperately needed their support.

It had only been a couple of days ago that she'd felt that way and yet so much had happened since then it felt like months. Now she was glad they were coming, not so much for the support and friendship they would offer but because they would be sharing in what was going to be one of the happiest days of her life.

Nerves fluttered in her stomach but she stead-fastly refused to give into them and headed to-wards the shower.

CHAPTER FOURTEEN

NADIR HAD NEVER been one to suffer from nerves and yet today, his wedding day, he was as jumpy as a stock trader facing his first day on the floor.

Maybe it had something to do with the overcast sky when normally it was true blue and cloudless this time of year. He gazed at the gathering cloud cover. The wind hadn't picked up enough to trigger a sandstorm so that was something at least. Especially since the convoy Nadir had sent out to find Zach had located the four-wheel drive he had been using overturned and buried in the sand. He hadn't told Imogen but he felt slightly sick at the thought that something sinister had happened to his brother. Fortunately no body had been recovered, which meant that he hadn't been buried along with the vehicle.

He knew he should probably call off the wedding until he knew what had happened but for some reason he couldn't bring himself to do it. He didn't think he'd properly relax until Imogen was truly his, which was ridiculous because she'd already agreed to marry him and she seemed happy about it. Or was she just making the best of a bad situation?

He frowned, recalling her slight hesitation the night before when he'd asked her if she was happy. She'd said yes and he had no reason to believe she was lying but that hesitation... Telling himself he was being paranoid, he counted off the other thing bothering him. The leadership position. For days now his mind had been vacillating over what to do about it and for a man who was used to making quick decisions that was just damned annoying.

His daughter bounced excitedly in his arms and he refocused his attention on the one area of his life he felt he had a handle on.

He had taken her early so that Imogen could relax in a deep scented bath and be prepared for him like so many brides had been prepared for their men in times gone by. He'd looked at her seriously and told her it was a tradition she couldn't refuse. She had laughed and said she was a girl and not only would she not refuse, but she'd revel in it while she was there.

That had set off all sorts of images in his head

about her naked and wet and smelling like the sweetest flower. Tasting like the sweetest flower.

Nadeena pointed to something over his shoulder and started babbling. 'What is it, *habibti*?' he asked before his mind wandered any further down the sex route. One night away from Imogen and he felt as randy as a teenager who'd just been given the green light to go all the way.

He turned in the direction of Nadeena's chubby finger and saw a young stable hand grooming a mare outside the stables.

'Hisaan,' he told her. 'Horse.'

He strode over to it and stroked its arched neck. His sister had loved horses and suddenly a picture of her materialised in his mind and guilt assailed him, as it always did when he thought of her. As it usually did when he felt happy.

'If this was Nadeena and she had made a mistake like the one you feel you made would you want her to punish herself for it for ever?'

She was smart, his Imogen, smart to strike right at the heart of the issue because of course he wouldn't want that for her. So why did he want it for himself?

He shook his head. As awful as that time had been, perhaps it was time he dealt with it and put it behind him. Of course he would change it if he could but he couldn't. But what he could do was take care of his own family. He could do what was right by them. Do what was right by Imogen.

He watched as his daughter gathered her confidence and reached out to place her hand against the horse's soft muzzle. The horse snorted a breath and she drew back, her wide eyes flying to his for reassurance. He gave it to her. Smiling and putting his hand back on the horse, encouraging her to do the same. 'It's okay, *habibti*. Nothing will happen to you while I have you.' His heart clenched as she followed his lead and then the skin on the back of his neck prickled. He glanced back towards the palace and saw Imogen watching them from the balcony of the temporary suite she had occupied the night before. Time seemed to stop and he couldn't take his eyes off her.

Her hair had been swept into an elaborate updo in preparation for the afternoon ceremony and her eyes were rimmed with kohl, her lips a deep pink. The honking of a car horn reminded him that stately cars had been coming and going all morning, delivering guests who would witness his joining with this woman he cherished above all others.

Cherished?

Loved.

He went dead still.

Was that really what was going on here? His heart pounded inside his chest as the words took root in his mind. He nearly laughed. Of course he loved her. It was as clear as crystal all of a sudden. His obsession with finding her, his uninterest in considering shared custody—and yes, he had strong views about that and he never wanted Nadeena to suffer as he had—but Nadeena wasn't him and neither he nor Imogen would do that to her.

He wiped a smudge of dirt from Nadeena's cheek. The simple fact was that Imogen completed him. Waking up beside her, holding her in his arms at night, listening to her talk about her dreams, her hopes…wanting to see her fulfil her true potential.

Last night she'd turned him away because she had wanted to start their wedding off on the right foot. Now he wanted to do the same thing. Because he knew she only wanted to marry for love and he wanted to tell her how he felt before the ceremony. He didn't want her going into this wedding thinking that this was nothing but a marriage of convenience for him. Or inconvenience, as he had arrogantly claimed a week ago. He gave his daughter a wry smile. 'Your papa can be an ass.'

She looked at him solemnly and babbled something as if she was in complete agreement.

Laughing, he glanced up at the balcony again only to find it empty. A sudden feeling of vulnerability gripped him hard. What would she say when he told her how he felt? And was now really the right time? Perhaps he should wait, sound her out a little before he dived straight in with the *I love you*s? Hell, how did a man even start a conversation like that?

Deep in thought as he strode into the palace, he didn't see his brother until he almost ran straight into him.

Relief was followed swiftly by absolute fury. 'Where the hell have you been? You have a lot of explaining to do.' He took in Zach's dishevelled state—his wrinkled clothes that were covered in dust and dirt, his beard growth that looked to be at least a week old.

'*I* do?' Zach raised a dust-covered eyebrow. 'Thanks for the concern and the belated rescue team.'

Nadir frowned. 'You look like hell. What happened?'

'The short version is that I had an unfortunate run-in with one of the less welcoming tribes in the mountains.'

'Hell. For a while I thought you were holed up with a woman.'

Zach laughed. 'I suppose technically you could say that I was but it wasn't by choice and she's more like a spitting she-cat than a woman. One who is currently locked in the old harem. Not the most convenient situation on your wedding day, but then I didn't know it was your wedding day until about an hour ago.'

Nadir stared at him. 'You have a woman locked in the harem?'

'Farah Hajjar, to be exact,' he growled, his words laced with disgust.

'Mohamed Hajjar's daughter!'

'One and the same.'

Nadir swore. 'Hajjar will have your head for that.'

Zach's gaze turned wry. 'They both very nearly did.'

'For the love of...' Nadir's gaze narrowed. 'You didn't compromise her, did you?'

His brother gave a sharp bark of laughter. 'A wild boar couldn't compromise that woman and nor would it want to.' His gaze fell on Nadeena. 'I take it this is my niece.'

'You're changing the subject.'

'I am.' He smiled at Nadeena. 'She's beautiful.'

'I know.' Nadir wanted to ask his brother what the hell had happened but there'd be time for that later. It was enough that he was back and in one piece. 'I don't have time to get the details now but you're okay.'

'No thanks to you,' he said without rancour.

'Ever heard of the boy who cried wolf? That will teach you for playing so many tricks as a kid.'

Zach grinned. 'Come chat while I get cleaned up.'

'I can't.'

'Why not? The wedding isn't for hours yet.'

'No, but…' Nadir shook his head. He wanted to see Imogen and it was all he could think about. 'Here, take your niece and get acquainted.'

He handed his daughter over and was surprised when Zach took her so easily.

'Hey, don't look so surprised. I'm okay with babies. They're like women and horses. Handle them with the utmost care and don't do anything to rub them up the wrong way. Isn't that right, *habibti*?'

Waiting just long enough to make sure his daughter wasn't going to start bellowing in protest, Nadir smiled when a little frown line materialised between her eyebrows as she reached up to touch Zach's beard. 'Don't let her cut herself on that and if she cries take her to Maab.'

'Where will you be?'

'With Imogen.'

'Ah.' His brother cocked his head and gave a knowing grin and Nadir took the stairs to Imogen's suite two at a time.

This time Imogen made sure she kept well away from the balcony doors. She shouldn't have gone out there before but the time since she had woken until now had been interminable. And she still had another four hours until the wedding.

Butterflies danced in her stomach and her lips felt dry again. At this rate she would go through the whole tube of Rose Delight Tasnim had given her before the ceremony even started.

She wasn't in her dress yet, just a silk robe that was part of a dowry Nadir had ordered for her. It was gorgeous Parisian silk, as was the under-

wear she had on. The dress too was beautiful. I
had been sewn by twenty local ladies and Tasnim
had told her they had worked around the clock to
create a dress fit for a queen. Which reminded
her that she wanted to pay for her own dowry
and she headed back inside and wrote a quick
note to herself. It was only a small thing but she
had started to wear the clothes Nadir had bought
for her and she didn't want him providing everything she needed.

She sighed and tried to find something else to
distract herself with because none of her old performance tricks seemed to do anything to settle
her pesky nerves.

Or was it anxiety? Was it because everything
had turned out so perfectly in the end? Or nearly
perfectly. Nadir had not told her that he loved her
but he cared for her and she believed that he would
always do the right thing by her and their children.

Imogen pressed her hand to her belly. Could
they have created another life together this week?

A knock on the door startled her and she knew
it was Nadir. She hadn't missed that searing look
he had given her from the courtyard or what it had
meant. The butterflies in her stomach flexed their
wings. He wanted her, that much was obvious, but

still a little gremlin of doubt managed to insinuate itself into her mind. *What if he'd changed his mind...? What if—?*

Mentally slapping the negative thoughts away, she marched over to the door. Even though she knew she shouldn't see him again before the ceremony, she didn't care. She needed the reassurance of his touch.

'Minh!'

Imogen burst into tears the minute she opened the door and saw her friend standing on the threshold dressed in a bespoke suit and tie, which he'd always said he would never wear.

'Imogen—' Minh stopped smiling and strode inside '—what's wrong?'

All the pent-up emotion of the last week spilled over and, even though she told herself not to cry because it would ruin her make-up, she couldn't seem to stop.

'Imogen, tell me what's wrong. If that bastard hurt you I'll deck him.' Minh took her into his arms and she shook her head to say that she was fine and buried her face against his chest. It was stupid to cry like this and she gave a hiccup and lifted her head, her smile tremulous. 'I'm sorry...I don't know what came over me. I've been waiting for you to get here and…oh, Minh, I'm just so—'

'Happy?'

Hearing Nadir's deep voice behind her, Imogen reared back from Minh and stared at Nadir. His face was closed. Hard. He raised an eyebrow. 'Ecstatic, even?'

Well, yes. She wiped beneath her eyes and her fingertips came away black. Oh, she must look a fright! 'I didn't hear you knock.' It was a stupid thing to say but the tone of his voice had thrown her mind into a spin.

'You left the door open.' His steely gaze scared her and then he cut his eyes to Minh. 'I need to speak with Imogen. Alone.'

'What have you done to her now?'

'Minh, don't.' Imogen had a sense of *déjà vu* but she knew by the expression on Nadir's face that something was very wrong. Had he received bad news about Zachim?

'I don't like this, Im. I told you—'

'Please, Minh. I'm sure this won't take a minute.'

Minh's reluctance to leave was as palpable as it had been back in London.

He threw Nadir a warning glare. 'I'll be right outside.'

Imogen breathed out when he closed the door behind him. She turned back to find Nadir by the arched windows, staring out. 'Nadir, what's wrong? Has something happened? Nadeena—'

'She's fine. I left her with Zach.'

'Oh, then he's back!'

'Yes.'

'That's wonderful news. I thought maybe, but...' She took a deep breath. Started again. 'Is he okay?'

'He's fine.'

She hesitated. 'So that's good. Isn't it?'

'It's very good.'

He turned and stuck his hands in the pockets of his jeans and stared at her.

'You're starting to scare me, Nadir.' She gave a soft laugh as if to alleviate the tension in the room but it just ratcheted it up even more.

'I'm sorry. I don't mean to.' He cleared his throat. 'But we need to clarify some things before the wedding.'

His voice was so devoid of emotion it made Imogen's stomach roil. 'Like?'

'Like the fact that you wouldn't be here if it wasn't for Nadeena.'

Her lashes came down to shield the hurt in her eyes. They both knew that was why he had brought her here. It wasn't news. So why was he mentioning it? Was he afraid she had twisted the reasons for their marriage into something it wasn't? Was he afraid she had fallen in love with him? Taking a deep breath, she tried to tell herself that everything was going to be okay. 'I know that.'

He nodded. 'And the fact that you never wanted this marriage.'

Imogen frowned. She half expected to see a gavel in his hand. 'No. I...' She hesitated, wondering how to answer when he jumped in first.

'Wanted to marry for love? Is that what you were going to say?'

She nodded and then shook her head. No, she hadn't been going to say that; she'd been going to say that in the beginning she had wanted that but now—

'Yes or no, Imogen?'

'Yes, I wanted to marry for love but...' She swallowed, her eyes searching his face for some clue as to what he was thinking or feeling. But this was the stranger Nadir—the man who had picked her up a week ago. The man who had walked out on her in Paris. A terrible premonition raised goose bumps along her arms but she pushed aside her apprehension and answered honestly. 'I've come to terms with that now.'

As if he'd somehow been waiting for that exact answer, he slowly raised guarded eyes to hers. 'Then you're free to go.'

'I'm sorry?'

'I said you're free to go.' He moved towards the door.

'Nadir...wait. I don't understand what you're saying.'

'I'm saying that I agree with you. A marriage of convenience is not a good enough reason to tie two people together for ever. Even for the sake of a child.'

'Hold on.' Imogen felt as if she had to fight to get every word out of her mouth. 'You're saying that you no longer want to marry me?'

'I'm saying you're free. You can leave.'

The room tilted and Imogen put her hand out to grip the back of a chair. Tears of disbelief spiked behind her eyelashes but she refused to let them fall. 'What about Nadeena?'

'My lawyers will be in touch about visitation rights—isn't that what they're called?'

Isn't that what they're called?

He was so cool and remote she wanted to scream. 'I meant—what about your desire to be part of her life? *Permanently.*'

Her body started shaking. This couldn't be happening. It just couldn't be happening.

'I still plan to be in her life. I just...' He looked away as if it was too difficult to look at her. 'I have reconsidered my position.'

He had reconsidered his position? As if they were nothing more than a piece of furniture he had decided he no longer wanted.

'Oh, my God!'

'I still want her,' he rasped harshly. 'But not this way.'

Stunned, Imogen could only stare at him, his words barely registering as her heartbeat raced out of control and her thoughts went along for the ride. All she could think was that he had changed his mind. 'I told you this would happen.' Suddenly she was fifteen again and her father was standing in the doorway and her mother was crying on the sofa. Thank God Nadeena wasn't old enough to witness her own humiliation at the hands of this man. She lifted her chin. 'Where's Nadeena now?'

'I told you she's with Zach.' He swiped a hand across his face but Imogen barely noticed.

'Damn it, Imogen. I thought you'd be happy.'

Imogen felt bile rise up in her throat but she held it back by sheer force of will, determined that he would not see how much he had hurt her again. How much she had *let* him hurt her again. God, she was an *idiot* of the most astonishing proportions. 'I am.'

He nodded. 'Then there's nothing left to say.'

'Nothing,' she assured him and sailed into the en suite bathroom before he saw the utter despair in her eyes.

Nadir sat behind his father's old desk, staring at his computer screen. When the door banged open he looked up and found his brother dressed in celebratory robes with a scowl on his face.

Zach didn't waste any time on niceties. 'What are you doing?'

'Working. You look better.'

'It's amazing what a shower and a shave will do.' Zach parked himself in the chair opposite the desk. 'Why are you working? You're getting married in less than two hours.'

Nadir focused on the email he'd been trying to read. 'Not any more. I've instructed Staph to send the guests home.'

'I know. He came to me.'

'Well, it's good that you're here. We need to discuss who will lead Bakaan and I've reconsidered my position. If you don't want the position then I'll be the next King.'

'Big turnaround.'

Nadir grimaced. 'It's amazing what can happen in a week.'

He'd found his ex-lover and his daughter, he'd fallen in love with them both and he'd lost them both. And taking on the role of leading Bakaan into the twenty-first century would keep him busy enough so that he wouldn't think of any of it.

'Nadir, bro…?' Zach used the kind of placatory tone he might if he was facing a band of militants with only a soup spoon to defend himself. 'I'm not sure that's the most important thing to discuss right now. What's going on?'

Nadir thought of the scene he had interrupted in Imogen's room. Her ex-lover holding her tightly in his arms.

At first he'd been furious, his instinct to grab hold of the smarmy buffoon and pull him off her and beat him to a pulp for daring to touch what was his. Then he'd registered that Imogen wasn't resisting. That she was snuggled against him and that she was weeping. Sobbing, almost.

Those tears had torn at his heart and he'd realised in a flash of unwelcome insight that he was behaving exactly as his father had done in stealing his mother from her tribal village in a fit of passion and then forcing her to bend to his will when he had taken another wife. Of course his circumstances were different from his parents, he knew that, but he also knew that the common denominator wasn't. He was a tyrant who hadn't given her a choice. He now had and she'd very definitely exercised it.

He forcibly shut his emotions down. He knew it had been a mistake to let them out. They had confused things. Made him think that sex was love when the truth was that he and Imogen shared a phenomenal chemistry and a child and he cared enough about her that he couldn't force her to do something she didn't want to do. 'Nothing is going on.'

Zach looked at him. 'Pull the other one—it has bells on it.'

Nadir cut him a brooding glare. 'Fine. I found Imogen in the arms of her ex-lover.'

'Naked!'

'No—' he heaved a sigh '—she was crying.'

Zach frowned. 'Why?'

'Because she wants to marry him, not me.' Nadir surged to his feet in irritation and turned towards the windows. 'How the hell should I know? Suffice it to say, she invited her ex-lover to our wedding and now they're together.'

Zach blew out a breath. 'That's rough. Why'd she do it?'

'I assume because she loves him.'

Zach nodded as if he fully agreed and then started shaking his head. 'No, I meant why did she agree to marry you when she's still in love with someone else?'

'Does it matter?' he asked briskly. 'The fact is she was living with this guy in London and now she's free to go back to him.'

Zach nodded again. 'Which she wants.'

'Right. Now, there's a lot to sort out. I'm hoping you want to stay on in Bakaan if you don't take the leadership role because I'm going to need a right hand and I want that to be you.'

'So, to be clear,' Zach began, completely ignoring his attempt to change the subject, 'she actually said that she preferred this other guy to your face.'

Nadir swiped a hand across his jaw. 'Can we just forget Imogen?' A muscle knotted in his jaw. 'She's not relevant to this discussion.'

'Sure.' Zach eased back in his chair. 'If you're happy with her bonking another guy then who am I to argue?'

Nadir slammed his portable mouse down on the desktop. 'I told you to forget her.'

'I will if you will.'

'Already done.'

'Nope.' Zach glanced at his feet. 'Must have left the bells in my rooms.'

'Dammit, Zach, I gave her a choice and she chose him. You want to rub my nose in it, you can go to hell.'

'Hang on a minute, buddy.' Zach surged forward in his seat. 'I'm not rubbing your nose in anything. I'm saying you might be wrong.'

'I'm not.'

'Then let me ask you this. Are you currently sleeping with her?'

Nadir stared at him, hard. 'You continue down this line of thinking and I can tell you it won't end well.'

'Just hear me out.' Zach threw up his hands defensively. 'I'm not trying to get a blow-by-blow description of your love life, I'm trying to say that I know women.'

Nadir scoffed.

'Scoff all you like, but I do, and I don't know many that would sleep with one guy while they were in love with another.'

Nadir eyed him coolly. 'They're out there.'

'Okay, sure, so what you're saying is that Imogen is one of those—'

'No, she's not. She would never play with people's emotions like that.'

'Right. So stop being a horse's arse.'

'Look, Zach, I know you're trying to make me feel better but you don't have to concern yourself. I'm good.'

'Bro, I'm not trying to make you feel better; I'm trying to talk you down off a ledge.'

'I'm not on a ledge.' Nadir's jaw hardened. 'The fact is I had no choice but to let her go. I forced her to come here. I forced the idea of marriage onto her and I wouldn't take no for an answer.'

'Like the old man.'

'Yeah.' Nadir blew out a rough breath. 'Just like the old man. Hell.' He stared at Zach bleakly. 'When did I turn into him?'

'You didn't.' Zach frowned. 'Admittedly, you're stubborn and a little on the arrogant side but you don't take advantage of people and you'd never step on someone else for your own gain.'

'That's where you're wrong.' Nadir stared at him bleakly. 'I stepped all over Imogen.'

Zach shook his head. 'I doubt that's true but if you did then go apologise and make nice. Tell her how you feel. See what happens.'

The thought of that made Nadir's gut pitch. He never told anyone how he felt. It was easier and no one got hurt that way. Least of all him. 'Hell. I love her.'

'You think?'

Nadir shook his head. 'I know you think you're pretty clever but frankly I wouldn't wish this sick feeling in my gut on anyone.'

'I would love to care for a woman as much as you do yours. Instead, I have to figure out how to stop myself from being shackled to a living, breathing fire-eater who would as soon run me through with a *kanjhar* than look at me.'

Nadir had forgotten all about Farah Hajjar. 'I doubt her father will push it. He hates our family.'

'It's fine. I can deal with Farah and her insane old man. You just do us both a favour and go get your woman.'

'Prince Zachim!' Both men looked up as Staph knocked and shot through the door like a rocket, his breath heaving. 'You need to come quick. The woman you put in the harem has disappeared.'

'Disappeared?' Zach frowned. 'That's impossible. I've put an experienced guard on the door.'

'Yes, My Lord. He can't find her.'

Zachim rattled off a string of curse words Nadir hadn't heard in a long while. He smiled and came around the desk. 'I'd love to stay and help but...'

His words faded as Zach, his mind already on the disaster that awaited him, strode out of the room.

Nadir headed for the door himself and stopped. 'Staph?'

'Yes, My Lord?'

'What did you tell the wedding guests who have already arrived?'

'Nothing, My Lord.'

Nadir gave him a faint smile. 'You're a sly old

dog, Staph. I hope your faith in me isn't misplaced.'

'I would say not, My Lord.'

'And Imogen and my daughter?' He cleared his throat. 'Where are they?'

'In your suite.'

Imogen sorted out what she would need for Nadeena for the plane trip back to London and searched around for some sort of bag to put it into. Nadir had luggage in his dressing room but no way was she going back into his bedroom ever again.

What he had said to her before...she still couldn't digest it because it felt as if he'd ripped a hole in her heart and inserted a stick of dynamite for good measure.

The only thing she was thankful for was that her daughter would never know how it felt to have an absent father because she would be used to having him part-time in her life and Imogen only hoped he would be good to her when he had her. That he wouldn't have a string of stick-thin models parading through his house who— Oh, God. Imogen felt her stomach heave and leant against a chest of drawers to steady herself.

It was so ridiculous to feel like this because she had known all along that once the reality of marriage and parenthood set in then he would run a mile and she'd been proven right. And the prize? She shook her head at her reflection in the mirror. Her prize was a broken heart the size of Asia.

'Imogen? *Habibi*? Are you all right?'

Imogen swung around at the sound of his voice, fire pouring out of her eyes. 'What are you doing here?'

He stopped short and she was thankful that she had wiped all her make-up off after her initial crying fit and dressed in her T-shirt and jeans. She intended to go home exactly the way she had arrived. Well, almost.

'I needed to see you.'

To make sure she was all right? She couldn't fault his manners. 'Well, now you've seen me, please go.'

'*Habibi*, I—'

'Do not call me *habibi*.'

'Okay—fine.' He held up his hands as if she were a wild thing about to pounce on him and maul him to death. What a pity, she thought, that shape-shifting was pure fantasy. 'I know I'm the reason you're upset and I just want to talk.'

'No.' Imogen shook her head for emphasis. 'No more talking. I'm done here, Nadir.'

He looked around the room and frowned when he saw the minuscule amount of clothing on the bed. The empty cot. 'Where's Nadeena? Isn't she due for a sleep?'

'Yes, but since we're leaving, Minh is trying to keep her awake so that she'll sleep on the—oh, this is not important. Could you please just go?' The last thing she wanted to do was break down and sob in front of him and the longer he stayed the more likely that was to happen. It was too painful to see him. Too painful to be near him.

He cleared his throat and shoved his hands into his pockets. 'It's probably good that we talk about him and get it out of the way.'

'Talk about whom?'

'Your friend, Minh.'

'What about him?'

He looked at her and his throat worked as he swallowed. 'Do you love him?'

Did she love him? 'Why are you asking me that?'

'Because I need to make sure I've done the right thing in letting you go.'

'Letting me go?' She shot him a fulminating

look. 'You told me to go. You've reconsidered, remember—you don't want to marry me.'

'Of course I still want to marry you. I only reconsidered the reason for our marriage.'

Imogen shook her head. 'You're not making any sense. You cancelled the ceremony.'

'Yes, but I didn't want to.'

'Then why do it?'

'Because you told me the reason you were marrying me was because we had Nadeena and I wanted more.'

'More?'

'Hell.' He swiped a hand across his face. 'I need to start again. What I'm trying to tell you is that I love you.'

'You love me?'

Her shock must have registered on her face because his expression turned grim. 'Yes, but if you prefer Minh then I'll walk away.'

'Nadir, Minh is gay.'

'Gay!' The look on his face was priceless and Imogen would have laughed if she hadn't felt so ill. Had he seriously thought that Minh was her lover? Looking back, she supposed he might have got that impression initially but... 'How could you think that I could be in love with him and make love to you?' she demanded hotly.

'As I explained to our daughter this morning, I'm an ass. Particularly where you're concerned. I can't seem to keep my head on straight when you're in the room and every male who looks at you sideways is a threat.'

'Are you serious?'

'Yes. If you knew how many ways I wanted to hurt them—'

'No.' She gazed up at him, not really daring to believe this was happening. 'The part about loving me.'

Nadir cupped her chin in his hand and kissed her deeply. Imogen moaned and pulled back. 'Stop that—it will only confuse things.'

'On the contrary, our physical relationship is the only thing that's not confused. Imogen, *habibi*, can you ever forgive me for being so stupid this afternoon? My only excuse is that when I saw you crying in the arms of your... friend I assumed it was because you didn't want to marry me and I couldn't bear the thought of hurting you.'

'But why would you think I didn't want to marry you?'

'Because I realised today that I'm more like

my father than I would like to think I am and
that I was forcing you to bend to my will and I
couldn't do it. I wanted to set you free, to give
you a choice.'

Imogen dashed at the tears on her face. 'I
thought you had decided that you didn't want me.
That I wasn't enough for you.'

'Oh, *habibi*, you're too much for me. You're too
wonderful, too beautiful, too giving. I'm pretty
sure I fell in love with you the minute I saw you
in Paris because I haven't been able to stop thinking about you since, only I didn't want to see it
because I was so afraid of getting hurt.'

Imogen sniffed back more tears. 'I'm guilty of
the same thing and oh, Nadir, I feel exactly the
same way. I fell in love with you the minute I
saw you and I've never stopped. I love you so
much it hurts.' Elation rushed through her until
she thought she might burst. 'Pinch me—I can't
quite believe this is happening.'

'Believe it,' he growled, pulling her in close
against him. 'And mark my words when I tell
you that there will be no more misunderstand-
ings between us. No more worrying about how
the other person feels. You know that I love you.

That I will always love you and whatever children we have. Tell me you believe me.'

'I believe you.' She grinned up at him. 'And not just because you command it to be so.' And then she turned serious because she knew she had to be just as open with him. 'I think part of the blame for today lies with me, though, because in my own way I saw what I expected to see and I didn't fight for you. I didn't fight for us. I won't do that again. I won't doubt either one of us again.'

'And I will never give you a reason to. Now, please, *habibi*, if you wouldn't mind giving me this?' He took her ring from her finger.

Then he got down on bended knee and Imogen didn't think she could love him more but, before he could ask her the question she knew he was about to, there was a noise in the doorway and she looked up to find Minh standing there with Nadeena, his eyes as big as saucers as he took in the scene.

'Ah, I think we'll come back.'

'No.' Nadir rose and swiftly crossed the room. 'I know we haven't formally met but I am Nadir Zaman Al-Darkhan and I would like my daughter, please.'

'Oh, right.' Minh blinked up at Nadir and Imogen thought he might swoon.

Then Nadir was in front of her again and taking up all her attention. He handed her Nadeena and then got down on one knee again. 'I'm glad our daughter is here because I want her to witness how a man should behave when he's in love with a woman so she will be in no doubt as to what to expect from a man in the future.'

'Oh, Nadir—' Imogen's nose tingled as tears formed in her eyes '—I love you so much.'

Nadeena clapped her hands and tried to reach for the ring Nadir held up but he shook his head. 'Sorry, *habibti*, this is for your mother.' Then he lifted his blue-grey gaze to hers. 'Imogen Reid Benson, will you please do me the honour of becoming my wife later this afternoon?'

'This afternoon!'

'Yes. Apparently there is a room full of guests waiting for us.'

'But I'm not ready!'

Nadir gave her a wry smile. 'Can I take that as a yes?'

'Yes, oh, yes. Most definitely yes!' She pulled him to his feet and stepped into his arms, where Nadeena promptly laid her head against his broad chest. Seeing it, Imogen did the same and Nadir cupped the nape of her neck and lifted her mouth to his.

'I think I need a tissue.'

Having forgotten all about Minh in the doorway, Imogen beamed him a wide smile. 'I'm getting married.'

Nadir brought her mouth back to his for one last searing kiss. 'Yes, you are. In an hour. And you should know that I've told Zach that I intend to become King if he doesn't want the position.'

Imogen smiled and finally felt that everything was as it should be in the world. 'He won't. You were born to be King, Nadir.' She reached up and ran her hand across his stubbled jaw, her eyes full of the love she felt for him. The love she would always feel for him. 'You were born to be *my* King.'

Nadir's smile was slow and sexy. 'A king who will be at your service. Always.'

* * * * *

MILLS & BOON®
Large Print – July 2015

THE TAMING OF XANDER STERNE
Carole Mortimer

IN THE BRAZILIAN'S DEBT
Susan Stephens

AT THE COUNT'S BIDDING
Caitlin Crews

THE SHEIKH'S SINFUL SEDUCTION
Dani Collins

THE REAL ROMERO
Cathy Williams

HIS DEFIANT DESERT QUEEN
Jane Porter

PRINCE NADIR'S SECRET HEIR
Michelle Conder

THE RENEGADE BILLIONAIRE
Rebecca Winters

THE PLAYBOY OF ROME
Jennifer Faye

REUNITED WITH HER ITALIAN EX
Lucy Gordon

HER KNIGHT IN THE OUTBACK
Nikki Logan

0615 Rom LP

MILLS & BOON®
Large Print – August 2015

THE BILLIONAIRE'S BRIDAL BARGAIN
Lynne Graham

AT THE BRAZILIAN'S COMMAND
Susan Stephens

CARRYING THE GREEK'S HEIR
Sharon Kendrick

THE SHEIKH'S PRINCESS BRIDE
Annie West

HIS DIAMOND OF CONVENIENCE
Maisey Yates

OLIVERO'S OUTRAGEOUS PROPOSAL
Kate Walker

THE ITALIAN'S DEAL FOR I DO
Jennifer Hayward

THE MILLIONAIRE AND THE MAID
Michelle Douglas

EXPECTING THE EARL'S BABY
Jessica Gilmore

BEST MAN FOR THE BRIDESMAID
Jennifer Faye

IT STARTED AT A WEDDING...
Kate Hardy

MILLS & BOON®

Why shop at millsandboon.co.uk?

Each year, thousands of romance readers find their perfect read at millsandboon.co.uk. That's because we're passionate about bringing you the very best romantic fiction. Here are some of the advantages of shopping at www.millsandboon.co.uk:

* **Get new books first**—you'll be able to buy your favourite books one month before they hit the shops

* **Get exclusive discounts**—you'll also be able to buy our specially created monthly collections, with up to 50% off the RRP

* **Find your favourite authors**—latest news, interviews and new releases for all your favourite authors and series on our website, plus ideas for what to try next

* **Join in**—once you've bought your favourite books, don't forget to register with us to rate, review and join in the discussions

Visit **www.millsandboon.co.uk**
for all this and more today!